The Cat Who
Wasn't a Dog

The Cat Who Wasn't a Dog

Marian Babson

Thorndike Press • Waterville, Maine

This Large Print edition is published by Thorndike Press®, Waterville, Maine USA and by BBC Audiobooks, Ltd, Bath, England.

Published in 2003 in the U.S. by arrangement with St. Martin's Press, LLC.

Published in 2003 in the U.K. by arrangement with Constable & Robinson Ltd.

U.S. Hardcover 0-7862-5963-9 (Mystery)
U.K. Hardcover 0-7540-7735-7 (Chivers Large Print)
U.K. Softcover 0-7540-7736-5 (Camden Large Print)

The text of this Large Print edition is unabridged. Other aspects of the book may vary from the original edition.

Set in 16 pt. Plantin.

Printed in the United States on permanent paper.

British Library Cataloguing-in-Publication Data available

Library of Congress Cataloging-in-Publication Data

Babson, Marian.
    [Not quite a geisha]
    The cat who wasn't a dog / Marian Babson.
      p. cm.
    Previously published as: Not quite a geisha.
    ISBN 0-7862-5963-9 (lg. print : hc : alk. paper)
    1. Women cat owners — Fiction.   2. London
(England) — Fiction.   3. Actresses — Fiction.
4. Widows — Fiction.   5. Cats — Fiction.   6. Large type
books.   I. Title.
PS3552.A25N67 2003b
    813'.54—dc22   2003049391

The Cat Who
Wasn't a Dog

Chapter One

If you ask me, Dame Cecile Savoy was overdoing it. Chewing the scenery, in fact. I'm as sympathetic as the next person — providing the next person isn't Evangeline — but she was beginning to set my teeth on edge.

I mean, widow's weeds were all very well in their day, I suppose, but I can't imagine where she'd even found any in this day and age. They must have been left over from some ancient theatrical production — *East Lynne*, perhaps. Especially that long, all-enveloping, rusty black cloak.

The draped black veil concealed her face. Judging by the whimpering snuffling noises coming from behind the veil, that was probably a mercy. From time to time, a black-gloved hand holding a black-bordered handkerchief slipped under the veil to dab at streaming tears.

Evangeline rolled her eyes at me and I rolled mine back. We were both trying to ignore the inert body in the pet carrier on the jump seat facing us. Dame Cecile had adamantly refused to allow it to be placed in the boot.

It was going to be a long day.

'Now then . . .' Eddie shut the door on us and climbed into the driver's seat. We had hired his taxi for the day to take us down to Brighton from London. 'Where to? The pet cemetery, is it? I don't have The Knowledge down 'ere. You'll have to tell me where —'

'Stuff Yours!' Dame Cecile said in a muffled voice.

'Eh?' Eddie turned to look over his shoulder at us. His eyebrows would have disappeared into his hairline, if he'd had a hairline. 'That's not very nice.'

'Stuff Yours!' Dame Cecile repeated.

'Now, now, Cecile,' Evangeline said between clenched teeth. 'We realize you're distraught and it's all terribly sad but, after all, the damn — er, the dear creature was about two hundred and fifty years old in human terms. It isn't as though it were cut down in its prime.'

'Stuff Yours!'

'In any case,' Evangeline decided to be pedantic about it, 'I believe the correct expression is "Up —"'

'Stuff Yours!' Dame Cecile trumpeted, in a voice that would have rattled the opera glasses in the chairbacks of the second balcony. 'Stuff Yours — the taxidermist, you fool!'

The day was going to be even longer than I had thought.

It had all started with that telephone call yesterday morning. Some day I'm going to train myself to stop answering the phone. But I had been expecting a call from my daughter, Martha, who had been hinting for days that she was soon going to have something wonderful to tell me — and so, I took the call.

'Hello? . . . Hello?' At first, I thought the person on the other end of the line was under water. The strange gasping, gulping, bubbling noises sounded more as though they emanated from a faulty water supply pipe in an aquarium than from any human source.

'*Ev— hoo-hoo — Evan— hoo-hoo . . . vangel— hoo-hoo . . .* sniff . . .'

'You want to speak to Evangeline?' I guessed wildly. 'Who's calling, please?' It didn't sound like a call she'd be delighted to receive.

'Let me talk to her!' The voice found itself and became almost coherent. 'I'm desperate! I need human warmth, sympathy, understanding . . .' it wailed.

'And you want Evangeline?' She must be desperate. Or else there was some other Evangeline in the city. 'What number are you calling?'

'Trixie! Stop playing the fool and put me through!' The momentary whiplash of command in the voice — which was beginning to sound familiar — was ruined by several more *hoo-hoos* and sniffs. 'This is an emergency!'

'On your head be it,' I muttered and called out, 'Evangeline, it's for you!'

'At this hour?' It was barely 10 a.m. and, although we were both up, we weren't really functioning yet — just sitting around waiting for the caffeine in the first cup of coffee to kick in enough to enable us to pour ourselves a second cup.

'She said she wants —' This was no time to repeat the warmth and sympathy routine. 'She wants to speak to you.'

Evangeline snatched the phone from me with a dirty look, as though I had been personally responsible for engineering the call just to annoy her.

'Who is it?' she snapped. 'Do you know what time it is? Or hasn't anyone explained the big hand and the little hand on the clock to you yet?'

Well, it was warm enough, I supposed, practically sizzling, in fact. But somehow I doubted that it was quite what the caller had had in mind.

Unusually for Evangeline, there was a long silence while the other person held forth. Even more unusually, Evangeline began to smile. It was not a pleasant smile. That was more like her.

'Oh, my poor dear Cecile,' she cooed unconvincingly, confirming my suspicion that it was Dame Cecile Savoy on the line. 'How too, too tragic for you. You mustn't worry about a thing at a time like this. Of course we'll do it for you.'

'What time like this?' I bleated. I didn't trust that smug look on her face for one second. 'What will we do?'

'Be quiet!' Evangeline snarled. 'No, no, not you, Cecile. Trixie, er, dropped a cup. So clumsy — and noisy. Do go on.'

I picked up the nearest dish and made threatening gestures with it. I *would* drop it — right on her head.

'Yes, yes, of course we will. Tomorrow, I promise. We'll be with you first thing in the morning. Er, that's when we'll start out. We should be with you by noon. No, no — don't thank me. What else could we do but stand by an old friend in her hour of grief?'

'What grief? What's happened?'

'Until tomorrow, then.' Evangeline replaced the receiver and turned to me with a triumphant light in her eyes. 'Trixie, we've got our play back again!'

'What play? What's going on?'

'*We're* going on! At the Royal Empire Theatre, Brighton, in the revival of *Arsenic and Old Lace* that was rightfully ours! The Show Must Go On — and Cecile is too distraught to step out on any stage for the foreseeable future. So you and I, Trixie, are going to step in and Save the Show!'

'Oh, no, we're not,' I said. 'We have our own brand new show being written for us!'

'Oh, yes.' Evangeline was momentarily abashed, 'I'd forgotten that in the heat of the moment.'

'What moment? What grief? Why can't Cecile go on?'

'Oh, she's lost that revolting little floor mop she was so attached to. Fleur-de-Mal, or whatever it was called, has finally popped her tiny clogs and Cecile is taking the whole thing rather badly.'

'Fleur-de-Lys has died?' I gasped. 'Oh, poor Cecile! No wonder she feels so awful. She adored that cute little Pekinese — and she'd had her practically for ever.'

'Exactly.' Evangeline poured her second

cup of coffee. 'There's no need for her to take on so. The thing has gone through about ten normal doggie lifetimes. I'd begun to think the damned creature was immortal. And so, I suppose, had Cecile.'

'And what's all this about tomorrow?' I persisted.

'I told Cecile we'd stand by her during the final rites.' Evangeline began to look more shifty than usual. 'After which, of course, we can go over to the theatre and get in some rehearsal time. They're opening in a week.'

'What do you mean, *we?* So Cecile can't — or won't — go on with the show. But what about Matilda Jordan? She's co-starring and I can't see her going into deepest mourning just because Dame Cecile has lost her dog. She'll still want to play her own part.'

'That's a point,' Evangeline admitted. 'We'll have to work on that one.'

'What we'll work on,' I said coldly, 'is getting Dame Cecile back on stage herself. We agreed it would be bad strategy to present ourselves as a pair of dotty old eccentrics and we've commissioned a bright new playwright to create a musical especially for us. Everything else apart, suppose we did do *Arsenic and Old Lace* and it was a big hit and we got stuck in a long run? We could lose the new show *and* the theatre Nigel is arranging for us. And I don't even want to think about Matilda Jordan's reaction to being dumped.'

'It *would* be a hit — with us in it.' Evangeline was weakening. 'But I'm sure Nigel could persuade his uncle to hold the theatre for us. He's such a dear helpful boy — and so misunderstood.'

'Mmmm . . .' In my opinion, people understood Nigel only too well. That was why he had lost most of the clients he had been financial adviser to. Mind you, so long as one didn't get financially involved with him, he was quite a pleasant chap and he did have an uncle with a jewel box of a theatre he'd kept dark for decades, but might be willing to release to us. But that was in the future and this was now.

'All right,' I said. 'We'll go down to Brighton and see Dame Cecile through her darkest hour — but we're going to persuade her to get back on that stage herself. No way are we going to get tied up in *Arsenic*. We have better things to do!'

'Stuff Yours,' Dame Cecile said. 'Here we are.' She gave a muffled sob.

Eddie pulled up in front of a dingy shop

14

sprawled across the end of a shallow cul-de-sac. Behind its grubby plate glass window, a variety of wild and domestic species were frozen for eternity in poses that were presumably typical of them in life.

'I can't go on,' Dame Cecile moaned, falling back against the seat. 'Not without my darling Fleur.'

I resisted a strong impulse to kick her out of the cab. Besides, it isn't so easy to do from a sitting position.

'Be brave, Cecile.' Evangeline rose to the occasion. 'Fleur would have wanted you to be.'

'That's true,' I chimed in. 'Fleur loved you dearly. She never would have wanted to think that she was causing you any pain.'

'Yes, yes, you're so right.' Dame Cecile mopped at her eyes and struggled forward in her seat. 'She was such a dear loving little darling. I must always think of her that way.'

'That's right,' Evangeline encouraged, adding, a little tactlessly I thought, 'Besides, you'll soon have her back again — even if not in quite the same form.'

Dame Cecile gave a heart-wrenching sob. Eddie opened the door and swung the pet carrier off the jump seat, which promptly snapped shut.

'Do be careful!' Dame Cecile cried.

'Why?' Evangeline asked. 'It can't hurt the — Ouch!' The hard push I gave her reminded her that she could still be hurt. She scrambled out of the cab with more haste than dignity.

'Place looks closed.' Eddie peered through the window into the deserted showroom.

'It can't be! They're expecting me!' Dame Cecile swept past him and rattled the doorknob. The door swung open and we stepped into gloom and silence.

'Sure you want to go through with this?' Eddie looked around uneasily and I didn't blame him.

We were surrounded by dead creatures. They stared at us with glassy eyes from dark corners. Birds perched on rocks beneath glass domes, a fox lurked in the shadows behind a trestle table, on top of which white mice paraded in increasing sizes from a baby mouse up to a large white rat. In a spotlit showcase in a corner was a Victorian tableau of baby squirrels enjoying a tea party. Beside the showcase, a hooded cobra coiled, ready to strike.

'Cor!' Eddie shuddered. 'This place doesn't 'alf give me the screaming 'abdabs.'

'And how!' I agreed. All those small

creatures that had once vibrated with life, now frozen for eternity in lifeless display chilled me. As well as those not so small: how could I have overlooked the horse dominating another corner of the room? Or the huge golden eagle, wings outspread, suspended from the ceiling?

Eddie deposited the carrier containing the late Fleur-de-Lys on the counter and shook his head.

'Where is Mr Stuff Yours?' Dame Cecile looked around impatiently. 'He promised he'd take care of me personally.'

Coming from him, that sounded more like a threat than a promise to me. Only Evangeline was unfazed.

'Shop!' She strode forward and thumped the old-fashioned bell on the counter, sending out a sharp *ping* to disturb the atmosphere and perhaps summon a shop assistant. 'Shop!'

The echo died away, the dust motes stopped dancing in the air, the place became quieter than ever.

'Maybe he forgot the appointment,' I suggested.

It was the wrong thing to say. Both Evangeline and Dame Cecile turned looks upon me designed to make me shrivel up and blow away. The honour of an appointment with one of the *grandes dames* of the British theatre was not to be forgotten by a mere taxidermist.

'Or else —' I remained firmly unshrivelled and standing my ground — 'something more important came up.'

'More important than Fleur?' *And me?* hung in the air. 'Don't be absurd! He knows how important this is.' *And I am!* 'He was so obsequious I thought grease was going to begin dripping out of my telephone. He would never —'

'Perhaps 'e left a note. "Back in five minutes" or something,' Eddie said. 'It could 'ave blown off the counter when we opened the door. Why don't we look around for it?'

'Good idea.' There was a half-open door immediately behind the counter: a sudden sharp draught could have sent a piece of paper flying through it.

I started in that direction. Eddie headed for a door at the far end of the showroom. Dame Cecile swept off her cape and handed it to Evangeline, in lieu of a maid. Evangeline looked at it incredulously and let it drop to the floor.

I detoured to pick up the cloak before Dame Cecile noticed — we'd had enough hysterics for one day — and continued on my way with it draped over my arm, leaving Dame Cecile and Evangeline wandering around the showroom peering vaguely into dusty corners.

The door behind the counter led into a very untidy office. Papers spilled out of filing cabinets and across a desk. The waste basket was overflowing. Any note that had blown in here was as good as lost, I might as well give up the search. That didn't mean I was ready to go back into the showroom quite yet. The silence in this room was not quite so oppressive and it was bliss to enjoy a few Garboesque moments alone. It might be my only chance all day.

I went behind the desk and sank down into the swivel armchair, letting my gaze rove around the office. It might be a mess, but it had something curiously soothing and familiar about it. Perhaps because half the agents and screenwriters I had known had had offices like this.

Well, perhaps not *just* like this. Tools of an unsettling and unfamiliar trade were also scattered around. I averted my gaze, not wanting to think about what they might be used for.

My attention was caught by the bough of a tree on a table in the far corner. Beside it was a wire cage containing a furry lump of some unfortunate animal. On the other side of that, an empty display case waited.

Curious, I got up and went over to it, even though my better judgement warned me that I might regret too close an inspection.

A typed white card was attached to the top of the wire cage:

CHO-CHO-SAN
Japanese Bobtail Cat

To be mounted on bough, left forepaw raised, head up and tilted to right side, tail semi-extended.

Deliver to:

The rest of the card had been torn off.

'Poor little Cho-Cho-San,' I sighed. 'You look so young and pretty. What happened to you?'

The bundle of tortoiseshell and white fur stirred and uncurled itself, two slanted gold eyes opened and stared up at me. She chirruped a pleased greeting.

'You're alive!' I gasped.

She blinked agreement and gave an almost apologetic little cough.

'But what are you doing here?' It was a silly question. The instructions for mounting attached to her cage had already provided that answer.

'But why?' Perhaps she was sick, dying — and some callous owner had brought her here to cough out the last of her life and be ready for . . . for . . . the moment she expired.

The bright eyes regarded me inquiringly, hopefully. She didn't look as though she were on her last legs.

Cautiously I extended a forefinger and poked it through the wire. She surged forward to rub against it enthusiastically. Her movement was smooth and fluid, her tiny nose was cold and wet, her fur was sleek and glossy, her eyes were bright and alert.

'You're not dying! You're not even sick!'

She chirruped agreement, cocking her head to the right to look up at me. She gave another delicate cough.

Then I smelled it, too. A strange nasty acrid smell and — over and above it — smoke.

' 'Ere —' I heard Eddie bellow from another room. 'There's a dead bloke in 'ere!'

A flickering red glow intensified at the back of one of the filing cabinet drawers. There was a crackling sound and grey smoke billowed out suddenly, followed by a shower of sparks and a burst of flame. At the same moment, I saw a dark wisp of smoke curl up from the laden depths of the waste basket.

'Fire!' I screamed. 'Fire!' Instinctively, I threw Dame Cecile's cloak over Cho-Cho-San's cage and swept it into my arms, running into the showroom.

'Get out of here! The place is on fire!'

Evangeline beat us all to the door, then had the nerve to act as though she was opening it for us.

'But what about the dead bloke?' Eddie emerged from the back room, took one look at the inferno erupting from the office and paled. 'Out!' he shouted. 'Out!'

'Fleur!' Dame Cecile wailed. 'My dear little Fleur! We can't leave her here!'

'It's all right!' Eddie grabbed Dame Cecile by the shoulders and propelled her through the door. 'Trixie's got 'er!'

Through the thickening smoke, Dame Cecile saw the bulky object in my arms, swaddled in her cloak, and allowed herself to be rushed into the open air.

We slammed the front door behind us and watched helplessly as the flames invaded the showroom.

'The fire brigade!' Evangeline dived for the cellphone in her handbag.

'Not you — they'll recognize your voice!'

Eddie grabbed it from her. 'They'd recognize any of your voices. We want the good old anonymous call. When they get the fire out and find that body they're going to start asking questions — and we don't have any answers.'

The crackle of flame and snapping wood was an effective background to Eddie's quick report to the fire brigade. We watched in stunned silence as the flames encroached more rapidly and virulently than we would have believed possible. It was all being destroyed so fast. Too fast. That nasty acrid smell must have been some sort of accelerant — and the fire had burst out of both the filing cabinet and waste basket. How many other spots around the shop had been booby-trapped?

'Right!' Eddie snapped off the cellphone and returned it to Evangeline. 'Let's get the 'ell out of 'ere!'

'Fleur! My little Fleur!' Dame Cecile tugged at the cloak covering the cage. I tugged back, trying vainly to keep it concealed. It was a losing battle against her infatuated determination. The cloak slipped and fell away.

Cho-Cho-San blinked with interest at the new world so suddenly revealed.

'Fleur!' Dame Cecile gave a piercing

scream. 'That's not Fleur! My baby is still inside! Being immolated!' She lurched towards the burning building.

'Ohmigawd!' Eddie snatched the cloak, hurled it over Dame Cecile's head and bundled her into the back seat. Evangeline and I dived in after her. Eddie leaped into the driver's seat and gunned the engine.

We sped away as the fire sirens sounded in the distance.

Chapter Two

At some point on that journey back to Dame Cecile's lodgings, a small paw slid through one of the wire squares of the cage and curled itself around my forefinger trustingly. I stroked it gently with my thumb as my heart melted. Who could have wanted to destroy such a little beauty?

There was nothing but an ominous silence from beneath the black cloak shrouding the figure slumped across the back seat facing us, as we perched on the jump seats.

'Cecile?' Even Evangeline was becoming uneasy. 'Cecile . . . are you all right?'

Silence.

'Cecile . . . we couldn't do anything else. The fire went out of control so fast. We had to save ourselves . . .'

Silence.

'Cecile . . .' I didn't reckon my chances, but felt duty-bound to weigh in. 'Cecile, there was nothing we could do for Fleur — but Cho-Cho-San was alive —'

That elicited a juddering sob. On the

whole, I preferred the silence.

'For God's sake, pull yourself together, Cecile!' Evangeline's always precarious patience snapped. 'Not even you can blame —'

Eddie slammed on the brakes as another fire engine careered out of a turning immediately ahead of us and swung in the direction of the conflagration.

I yelped, hanging on to the cage, as I slid forward in the seat. Cho-Cho-San gave a ladylike yowl, extending and quickly retracting her claws. Evangeline's snarl of protest mingled with Eddie's ripe curses.

Still silence from Cecile. Even though the black-shrouded form slithered about, nearly falling off the seat.

Evangeline and I settled back in our jump seats, exchanging glances. At this point, it was probably too late to try to do anything about the seat belts, even if they had been designed to accommodate a supine figure, rather than a sitting passenger. Anyway the fire engine had passed and, with luck, we would not encounter another one. We were rapidly moving beyond the vicinity of the blaze.

Silence. I couldn't even hear her breathing. I could only presume that she was.

I looked at Evangeline, who shrugged,

rolled her eyes heavenwards, and washed her hands of the whole proceedings.

Well, she knew Dame Cecile better than I did. I took a deep breath and told myself that the cloak was not wrapped around the Dame so tightly that it would cut off her breathing.

I hoped.

' 'Ere we are.' Eddie drew up in front of the Regency townhouse and turned off the engine. 'Home at last, eh?'

Silence. Deep silence.

'Anyone getting out?' Eddie's nerves were beginning to fray. Join the club, Eddie.

'I am!' Evangeline swung open the door on her side and leaped out. I opened my door and followed more slowly since I had Cho-Cho-San to cope with.

Still silence. No reaction at all from the motionless form lying along the back seat.

'Ohmigawd!' Eddie moaned. 'Do I 'ave to carry 'er?'

'Do as you see fit!' Evangeline was already half-way across the pavement, leaving no one in any doubt that she had done all that she was going to.

I trailed after her, with an apologetic glance towards Eddie, but he could see that I had my hands full.

Cho-Cho-San crouched low in her cage, eyes wide and apprehensive. She looked up at me pleadingly.

'It's all right, darling,' I soothed. 'You'll never see anything like that terrible place again. You're safe now.'

Behind us, I heard Eddie swearing in a deep steady monotone, punctuated by a series of thumps.

I steeled myself not to turn around. I didn't want to know. Especially not when I heard a sudden hysterical shriek.

Evangeline had no such qualms. I saw her turn around and a slow grim smile spread across her face.

I would not look . . . I would not look . . . I would —

Eddie was advancing relentlessly, a squirming black bundle locked in his arms. Upside-down evidently, since two legs were kicking wildly above his head — and the stubborn silence was now broken by a series of breathless gasps, shrieks and muffled imprecations.

'Open the door!' Eddie choked, reeling up the front steps. 'For Gawd's sake, open the door and let's get her inside before the neighbours call the police!'

'Has she got the key?' Evangeline demanded. 'Turn her upside — Well, shake her and see if the key falls —'

I put out one hand and twisted the knob. The door swung open.

'It wasn't locked,' I pointed out unnecessarily.

'Thank Gawd for that!' Eddie staggered through in front of us, aimed himself at the drawing room and dumped his burden down on the red plush sofa.

It immediately went limp and silent again. Perhaps the nasty thump I heard as it connected with the wooden frame had something to do with that.

'There! I've done my bit.' Eddie glared at us accusingly. 'And then some! It's over to you now.'

I headed for a capacious armchair, balanced the cage on one wide arm, sank into the seat and fiddled with the catch until I managed to release it and open the door.

Cho-Cho-San surged out of the cage and into my arms. She clung to me, shivering and uttering small mewls of distress.

'Shhh . . . shhh . . . it's all right.' I cuddled her. 'You'll never have to go back into that horrible thing again.'

Which reminded me. I glanced across at the dark lump on the sofa. 'Shouldn't we unwrap her?'

'If you must,' Evangeline sighed. She had settled into the opposite armchair and was studying her fingernails. 'On your heads be it, though.'

'Well, we can't just leave her like that,' I protested.

'Why not?'

'Ohmigawd!' Eddie was leaning against the mantelpiece, mopping his brow. 'Who's going to do it?'

Silence.

Don't all rush to volunteer.

Who'll bell the cat? Cho-Cho-San had moulded herself against me and was beginning to throb with a small weak purr. I wasn't going to disturb her now that she was settling down. I held her closer, stroking her, comforting myself as much as her.

'She's dead quiet,' Eddie said uneasily. 'You think, maybe, she 'it 'er 'ead when I dropped 'er on the sofa?'

'As long as it was just her head,' Evangeline said, 'there's no damage done.'

There was an ominous twitch beneath the cloak.

' 'Ere —' Eddie said. 'I think she's coming round.'

'Where do you suppose —' Evangeline stood and looked about the room speculatively — 'they hide the brandy around here?'

'Good thinking,' Eddie approved. 'That ought to 'elp —' He broke off abruptly as Evangeline found the bottle, poured a generous dollop — and proceeded to drink it herself.

The black bundle began to flail about frantically. Dame Cecile had known Evangeline longer than any of us. She had no illusions as to what was happening.

'Here —' Since Eddie obviously felt that he was far too involved already, I gave up. I decanted Cho-Cho-San into his arms and stepped forward to disentangle the Dame.

It wasn't easy. All that thrashing around had twisted the material tightly around her. There was also the very real danger of a black eye if I got too close to those thrashing limbs. I tugged tentatively at a loose bulge in the cloak, but stepped back hastily as a wildly flailing fist appeared from beneath it and just missed me.

Evangeline had been watching critically. Now she drained her glass, set it down on the coffee table and took centre stage.

'You'll never get anywhere that way,' she said. 'You need to treat it like one of the old adhesive bandages. A quick sharp pull and —'

She caught up a loose end of the cloak and gave it a sudden upward yank and

31

twist. Dame Cecile went spiralling off the sofa to land all of a heap on the floor.

My dears, the language! Poor Eddie cringed — although he could dish it out, he couldn't take it, especially from a woman. If he hadn't been holding Cho-Cho-San, I believe he would have put his hands over his ears. If he'd had enough hands he'd have covered Cho-Cho-San's ears, too. She was far too young and innocent to listen to that sort of thing.

'That's the way to do it!' Evangeline regarded Dame Cecile with satisfaction. 'Up you get, Cecile, and play hostess. In case you haven't noticed, you have guests. Start pouring the drinks.'

'I will never forgive you!' Dame Cecile choked. 'Never!'

Only Eddie looked worried. I retrieved Cho-Cho-San and sat down.

'Fix your hair, Cecile,' Evangeline said. 'As it is, you could step straight onstage as *The Madwoman of Chaillot* right now.'

'Never! Do you hear me? Never!' Dame Cecile struggled to her feet, glaring at Evangeline. 'And you can forget any idea of replacing me in *Arsenic and Old Lace*. I shall go on with the show myself!'

Thank heaven for that. I exhaled a silent sigh of relief. Although I thought I had

Evangeline fairly well convinced that she shouldn't take on the role, it was a relief to know that it was no longer available.

'Mine's a brandy,' Evangeline said. 'Trixie? Eddie? Cecile is waiting.'

'Brandy is fine with me.' I was abruptly aware that I could use something bracing.

Eddie nodded agreement weakly. The adrenaline rush had faded and the aftermath was beginning to affect us all. I don't know if Eddie felt as limp as I did, but his face was pale and he was shuddering sporadically.

I leaned back and closed my eyes, but a vision of exploding flames shot up behind them and I opened them again. Cho-Cho-San looked up at me meaningfully, then began licking at her ash-spattered front.

She was right, she was a mess; we were all a mess. Flecks of soot had smudged every face and settled on our clothing. Even as I watched, a large flake drifted off from Evangeline's sleeve and settled on the white carpet. I noted in passing that she appeared to have a double set of eyebrows and Eddie's streaks around the ears would have passed for muttonchop whiskers from a seat in the stalls. I didn't want to think what my own face must look like. It was time I got to a mirror — and a wash basin.

Even Dame Cecile had not escaped. The

cloak had obviously trapped a cloud of cinders as Eddie had whirled it over her and I decided I'd rather not be around when she discovered the tiny singed holes dotting her silk gown.

'I think I could do with a little freshening-up.' I lowered Cho-Cho-San to the floor and stood up carefully, trying not to smear the arms of the chair with my sooty hands. 'We all could.'

'Cor, you're right. Soon as I finish this drink, I'll do something about it.' Eddie spoke for us all as we reached for the drinks Cecile was sulkily passing around.

'Cor!' Eddie swallowed half of his drink in one gulp and shuddered. 'That was a close one!'

'Immolated!' Dame Cecile wailed suddenly, almost causing me to drop my glass. 'My little Fleur — immolated!'

'According to Eddie, she wasn't the only one,' I said. 'There was a human body in the back room. A dead one.'

'Ohmigawd!' Eddie gulped the other half and tottered over to the drinks table to refill his glass. 'Can't you forget that?'

'I suppose you're sure he *was* dead?' Evangeline could always be relied on for a happy thought.

'Ohmigawd!' Eddie whirled on her.

'Don't you start! That's it — go and wash your faces. I'm taking you back to London!'

'Sounds good to me.' I was more than ready to shake the dust — and ashes — of this place off my feet.

'You can't go now!' Dame Cecile was wailing again. 'You can't desert me when I'm bereaved and in a state of shock and have a show opening in a week.'

'For once in her life, she's right,' Evangeline said. 'We can't leave her. She needs moral support.'

'If she's expecting anything moral from you two, she's in trouble,' Eddie muttered.

'What was that?' Evangeline turned on him dangerously.

'Nothing. Forget I spoke.' Eddie could recognize defeat when it was staring him in the face. He poured himself another drink and raised the glass to us. 'Cheers!'

'I've forgotten my lines!' Dame Cecile shrieked. 'I can't remember a single word.'

'You never could,' Evangeline said. 'Have another drink. It will be all right on the night.'

'It won't! That's the biggest lie in show business!' Dame Cecile was a quivering mass of hysteria. 'My hair! My face! My lines! My Fleur — my poor dear little Fleur. She was my luck, my mascot, my friend! I can't go on without her!'

'Well, we're not going on!' I was getting cross. The least she could do when she issued an ultimatum was stick by it. If she was never going to forgive us, why did she want us to hang around?

'Whatever we do,' Evangeline said, 'I suggest we have lunch first. It's been a full morning and I, for one, am starving.'

Lunch? Incredulously, I consulted my watch. She was right. Although the day seemed to have gone on for ever, it was really only one thirty. Come to think of it, I was getting quite hungry myself.

'Blimey, I could eat a horse!' Eddie agreed fervently.

'No! I'm not hungry!' Dame Cecile was off again. 'I couldn't eat a thing! Not when —'

'You must eat to conserve your strength!' Evangeline met declamatory style with declamatory style. 'You have a Duty to your Public!'

'Yes . . .' Dame Cecile allowed herself to be persuaded. 'I suppose you're right.'

'That's settled!' Eddie said decisively. 'Now, in or out?'

'What?' Dame Cecile was momentarily bewildered.

'Do we go out to eat or do we eat 'ere?' Eddie asked. 'Like, where's the kitchen?'

'How do I know?' Dame Cecile glared at him. 'This is Matilda Jordan's house. I'm a guest here while we're rehearsing and then for the run of the play. So much more convenient than going back to London every night.'

Run-of-the-play sounded quite grand if you didn't know that the Royal Empire's presentations were usually limited runs for plays on their way to somewhere else, either the West End or a provincial tour.

'Come along, Trixie.' Evangeline was half-way to the door, with Dame Cecile not far behind her. I started forward automatically, then hesitated as I heard a faint anxious meow from somewhere around my ankles. I looked down into a pair of reproachful eyes. I had forgotten the cat.

'Bring 'er along,' Eddie said. 'She can stay in the cab while we eat and we'll get 'er a doggie bag.'

A slight shudder seemed to shake the delicate frame, the eyes pleaded with me.

'I think she's been moved around enough,' I said. Who knew where she had been and what had happened to her before she wound up in the chamber of horrors that had been Stuff Yours? 'She's frightened, she might run away if she got outside.'

'Wouldn't that be a shame?' Evangeline muttered.

'I'll stay here with her until you people get back,' I said firmly. 'Maybe I'll even find the kitchen. If you think Matilda Jordan wouldn't mind.'

'Help yourself,' Dame Cecile said. 'Matilda won't even notice. She has more to worry about right now than a bit of food.'

'Oh?' Evangeline was suddenly agog for anything that promised gossip or, preferably, scandal. 'Anything we should know about?'

'Family and theatre.' Dame Cecile sighed deeply. 'We're having trouble with our Teddy Roosevelt. He's hopeless! He keeps uttering the *"Charge!"* as though the next words were "to my account".'

'Too late to replace him?' This was a problem Evangeline could really sympathize with. 'Or a watertight contract?'

'Worse! He's the director's husband.'

'Cor! You are in trouble.' Even Eddie could see the difficulty.

'Who's directing?' Evangeline asked.

'Frella Boynton.'

'Oh? Didn't she — ? Is *he* the one?'

'Yes. So, you see, she can't now —'

'Of course not.'

They nodded solemnly at each other. They knew what they were talking about, even if no one else did.

It drives me crazy when Evangeline takes off like that with one of her old cronies. The only way to find out what they're talking about is to pretend utter indifference. I stooped and picked up Cho-Cho-San, fussing over her, to her delight.

'Right!' Eddie said. 'Food first, everything else later.' He led them out and, after a moment, I heard the taxi start up.

'Shall we explore?' I carried Cho-Cho-San towards the back of the house, that was usually where kitchens were located.

Sure enough, right where it was supposed to be. A bright cheerful room with a back door opening on to a small deck with a cluster of green-and-white garden furniture. There were steps at the end leading down to a lawn bordered with flowerbeds. Very nice, especially with the blue sky and sunshine. Perhaps, when I'd found something to eat, I'd take it out on the deck to the table under the big umbrella.

The kitchen was a bit old-fashioned, but nothing wrong with that. In fact, I preferred it. After the ultra high-tech monstrosity dominating our Docklands flat, it was a pleasure to be in a kitchen where I felt I could safely push a wrong button without the fear of being hurled into outer space.

There were even pots of herbs on the windowsill over the sink. I recognized chives, basil, parsley, dill and coriander — all looking a bit sorry for themselves.

'You poor things!' I watered them hastily and they began to perk up visibly. The basil released a cloud of fragrance, as though in thanks.

The fridge was sparsely stocked, but I found a compartment holding eggs, a dab of butter and a hardened chunk of Parmesan cheese. Purring almost as happily as Cho-Cho-San, who had jumped up on a chair and, forepaws on table, was supervising, I shaved off a couple of tablespoons of Parmesan and tore up a few basil leaves to add zip to the scrambled eggs.

We were both so absorbed that we didn't hear her enter. There was just a sudden apparition in the kitchen doorway and a Voice of Doom demanding:

'What are you doing with Cho-Cho-San?'

Chapter Three

'You know her?' It was immediately apparent that that was a dumb question. Cho-Cho turned her head and greeted the woman with a friendly little chirrup.

'What is she doing here?' The woman strode over to scoop Cho-Cho into her arms and glared at me accusingly. 'What are *you* doing here? Who are you? Are you Matilda's new housekeeper?'

Oh, fine. So much for fame. Perhaps it had been longer than I thought since that last movie. Or perhaps Job wasn't as good at publicity as he claimed.

'Who are you?' I countered, although it was clear that she must have a strong connection with Cho-Cho-San, who had settled unprotestingly in her arms. So strong that I didn't really want to explain what I was doing with the cat — nor where I had found her.

'I am Soroya Zane!' She drew herself up dramatically, waiting for a reaction she didn't get. She didn't know me. I didn't know her. We were even.

'And Cho-Cho-San is my cat,' she finished, somewhat deflated.

I nodded glumly. I'd been afraid of that.

She obviously gave me up as a bad job and diverted her attention to the table, looking down at the ingredients for my lunch.

'That will do,' she said grudgingly. 'I suppose one can't expect too much while you're settling into the job. I'll want toast and black coffee with it. You can serve me in the dining room.' She turned and stalked out of the kitchen. I still didn't have the faintest idea who she was.

Or even what she was. Judging from her outfit and improbable name, she might be telling fortunes in a booth down on Brighton Pier. If they still had fortune tellers on piers, that is.

I looked down at my own outfit. Soroya definitely looked like an over-the-top fortune teller, but did I look like a housekeeper? In deference to Dame Cecile's bereavement, I had worn a long-sleeved classic black dress, the sort you're supposed to be able to dress up or dress down. Obviously, I had gone too far in the down direction.

In a thoroughly bad mood, I slammed a frying pan on the hob and hurled a scrap of butter into it. I was going to have my own lunch and Madame Soroya, or whatever she wanted to call herself, could wait in the dining room until hell froze over.

Only . . . Cho-Cho-San was probably starving after her ordeal and she had looked so happy at the prospect of scrambled eggs and sniffed so delightedly at the Parmesan. If she had been a dog, she would have wagged her tail. But she was a cat. A hungry cat. Soroya's cat.

Relenting, I made toast, then piled the scrambled eggs on to it, except for a couple of tasty spoonfuls I put into a saucer for Cho-Cho-San. At the last moment, I wondered whether I should have cooked them more plainly for her.

'What's this?' But it was Soroya who poked her fork suspiciously at a fragment of green leaf, while Cho-Cho-San dived happily into her saucer.

'Basil — you'll find it's delicious,' I ordered grimly.

'Where's the coffee?' A hesitant mouthful had told her she couldn't complain about the eggs, so she looked for something else to moan about.

'Coming up!' And dumped right over your head if your manners don't improve! I stalked back to the kitchen and began shredding more basil for myself while waiting for the kettle to boil. Instant would be good enough for her.

A neat little pile of Parmesan shavings joined the heap of torn-up basil leaves before the kettle finally boiled. I threw a double portion of instant coffee granules into a cup, sloshed in the water and carried it into the dining room.

I didn't expect any thanks and I didn't get any. Before she could think of another complaint, I wheeled about and returned to the kitchen. Just inside the door, I stopped dead.

Another woman stood by the kitchen table, looking down thoughtfully at the eggs. Where were all these people coming from? I'd thought Dame Cecile was the only house guest.

'Oh!' The woman became aware of me and was momentarily startled before recovering herself. 'Are you — ? Yes, this will do nicely for lunch. It looks rather good.'

'Doesn't it?' I got the feeling that there went my lunch again. I should have gone out to a restaurant with the others.

Still looking faintly puzzled, the woman nodded and crossed to the door leading into the dining room. She started to go in, then recoiled violently.

'What's *she* doing here?' The force of her

44

recoil had carried her half-way back across the kitchen, to face me accusingly.

Eating my lunch. I shrugged. 'I don't know. I thought she lived here.'

'Never!' She reared back and glared at me. 'I don't know how you could have thought that. I distinctly told you at the interview that —' She did a double-take. 'You're not Mrs Temple! Who are you? What are you doing here?'

'At the moment, I seem to be a short-order cook.' The eggs were done and I slid them on to a plate and went back to the fridge for the last two, wondering if I had a chance at them this time.

'God, my head aches!' She slumped into a chair at the table and began to pick at the eggs. 'Why does she have to come back now? I can't cope. I just can't cope!'

'Hangover?' I was sympathetic. At least she hadn't asked for toast. Perhaps she was on a diet.

'If only!' She dropped her fork and buried her face in her hands. 'It's all too much!'

Unprompted, I set a cup of coffee beside her plate.

'Thank you.' It was hot, but she drank half of it before replacing the cup in the saucer and looking at me as though she were really seeing me. 'I've placed you now. You're Trixie Dolan!'

'And you're Matilda Jordan.' I'd recognized her, too. Any lingering doubt had been dispelled the moment she'd opened her mouth. She had one of those warm, low, clotted-cream voices guaranteed to keep an audience enraptured even through a reading of the telephone directory.

'Then it's true! You're taking over Cecile's part. At least,' she amended cautiously, 'Evangeline Sinclair is.'

'Relax,' I told her. 'Evangeline has worked her usual magic and driven the Dame into such a state of fury that she'd go onstage if she had to crawl, just to keep Evangeline from playing the part. The show will go on as scheduled.'

'Oh!' She closed her eyes briefly, then disposed of the rest of the coffee. 'Then what — ?'

She broke off as Cho-Cho-San strolled into the kitchen, heading for me hopefully.

'Where did that cat come from? What is it doing here?'

'Soroya says it's hers.'

'She's lying!'

'Really?' I brightened. That was the best news I'd heard all day.

'Well, perhaps not really. But she thinks

46

it's hers. She thinks everything is hers — or ought to be. She's a bit of a fantasist, I'm afraid. That cat is no more hers than it is yours.'

My spirits plunged again. She needn't have gone that far. Cho-Cho-San was weaving herself around my ankles, re-minding me, as though I'd need reminding, that she was there and still hungry and would appreciate a bit more to eat.

I bent and stroked her absently. I didn't quite have the nerve to rummage through the fridge for leftovers now that the lady of the house was sitting there watching us.

'Hungry, darling?' I hinted strongly. 'Want your lunch, too?'

'Oh — open a tin of fish for her.' Matilda could pick up on a cue. 'There are some small tins in the —'

'You may clear the table now!' Soroya ordered grandly, appearing in the doorway, mistress of all she surveyed. Until she real-ized Matilda was in the room, when she deflated slightly, but held her ground, waiting for me to leap to her command.

'She isn't the housekeeper, Soroya,' Matilda said between clenched teeth. 'She's a friend of Cecile's.'

'Indeed?' That obviously did nothing to recommend me to Soroya. 'Then what is she doing cooking meals in the kitchen?'

It was a fair question. I just didn't feel up to answering it. I looked to Matilda, but her eyes were closed and she seemed to be concentrating on breathing deeply.

'Well?' Sensing weakness, Soroya aimed her guns at me. 'What are you doing here, making free with my cat — and upsetting my daughter?'

Daughter? Soroya might be well into middle age, but she still had to be at least fifteen years younger than Matilda. Maybe twenty.

'I am not upset.' Matilda opened her eyes and stared at the remains of her congealing eggs.

'Of course you are! Look at you. You're pale as death. And that vein in your forehead is throbbing — you're getting a headache. This woman, whoever she is, is upsetting you.'

I could think of a lot of reasons why Matilda was upset, but I wasn't one of them. Soroya, on the other hand . . .

'Soroya, this is Trixie Dolan.' Matilda appeared to remember her manners. 'Trixie, this is . . .' She hesitated, took another deep breath, and bit the bullet. 'This is Soroya . . . Jordan. My stepmother.'

Why was I surprised? I'd seen enough of

over the years in Hollywood. It was par or the course. As long as they could be propped up enough to stagger into the Registry Office, some men were going to keep on marrying, collecting trophy wives like custom-built cars, turning them in for a newer, more up-to-date model every couple of years. The brides, of course, got younger every year, until they were marrying the equivalent of their fathers or, in some extremely well-heeled cases, their grandfathers. Money talks, especially pillow talk.

'How do you do?' I wasn't going to shake hands. I nodded coolly, not that I thought Soroya could recognize such fine distinctions.

'I thought you were out of the country, Soroya,' Matilda said delicately. 'When did you get back?'

'Just a few days ago.' Soroya waved a hand vaguely. 'I had business in London but, when I saw that you were about to open in a new show, of course, I put it aside and rushed down here. You need your family supporting you at a time like this.'

'And you just happened to have the key to my house.' This was obviously a sore point. 'So you didn't even bother to ring up and let me know you were coming.'

49

'I didn't want to bother you, dear.' C
from the expression on Matilda's face, give
her time to change the locks. 'You need to
concentrate on your lines and not worry
about running around tidying my house
before I arrive.'

'It's *my* house!'

'Oh, I know your father always allowed
you the run of the place — and I haven't
changed that, have I? I know you take good
care of it.'

'My father had nothing to do with this
house. It's mine! I bought it with my own
money. He had no claim on it at all.'

'I'm sure you've managed to convince
yourself of that over the years.' There is
nothing more maddening than a forgiving
smile from someone in the wrong to
someone in the right. Matilda went such a
terrifying shade of puce that I thought
Evangeline might have to appear at the
Royal Empire after all. I only hoped
Matilda wouldn't be appearing at the
nearest operating theatre.

'Now you mustn't get wrought up over
trifles.' Even Soroya had noticed. 'I'm not
planning to evict you. I'm quite content to
leave things as they are. You've been an excellent caretaker of the property while I
have pursued my career in India. In fact —'

Soroya swooped and picked up Cho-Cho-San, then wheeled towards the door, throwing her exit line back over her shoulder:

'In fact, it has been quite a comfort to me in times of stress to know that you're keeping your father's legacy safe for me until I choose to retire here.'

Cho-Cho-San looked to me in bewilderment as she was carried from the room. We heard footsteps beginning to ascend the stairs.

'I'll kill her!' Matilda choked. 'I swear, some day I'm going to kill her!'

Chapter Four

No jury on earth would have convicted her. Any right-minded person would have felt the same. It was rather a pity that she didn't actually mean it.

'My father's legacy!' the famous voice gurgled, half-way between a laugh and a sob. 'She's the only legacy I had from him — another millstone around my neck. Just to make sure that I really miss him!' She pushed her plate aside and buried her head in her arms on the table, small semi-hysterical gurgling noises still coming from her.

'Just because she said she wouldn't evict you,' I tried to cheer her, 'doesn't mean you can't throw her out.'

'Oh, no?' Matilda lifted a tear-stained face. 'That wasn't a promise — that was a threat. She's on her best behaviour because you're here to witness it. She was reminding me that, if I tried to get rid of her, she'd call a press conference and denounce me. And wouldn't the tabloids love that?'

They certainly would. I shuddered.

They'd tear Matilda apart, resurrect old scandals — why was I so sure that Soroya and Matilda's father would figure prominently in them? — and generally have a field day at her expense and possibly the expense of the play.

'My father's legacy!' Matilda said bitterly. 'She was only married to him for the last three years of his life — the old fool! She soon found out he wasn't the catch she thought he was. I don't see how she can imagine he had anything to leave.'

There wasn't much I could say to that. I made what I hoped were soothing and sympathetic little noises and wondered how long it would be before the others got back. Maybe I could remember an urgent appointment someplace else.

'To be fair,' Matilda said reluctantly, 'I suppose he did tell her the house belonged to him. He lied about everything else, why not that?'

I made more noises. And people think Hollywood kids had it tough! I guess the children of any actors anywhere have a lot to contend with. But some of us have a better grasp on reality than others.

'Oh, well,' Matilda was talking herself into a better mood, 'at least she isn't around too often. Her work keeps her out

53

of the country most of the time. And I can't see her ever retiring — she likes all the attention too much. Of course, she might fall out of favour, or be supplanted by another actress, but I'll cross that bridge if I come to it.'

'Actress?' Had I missed something? I'd thought I was pretty well up to date in what was going on in the profession and who was who. 'I'm afraid I didn't recognize . . . ?' A likely thought struck me. 'Perhaps she's on permanent tour as Madame Arcati in *Blithe Spirit*?'

'Better than that.' Matilda was definitely seeing the silver lining now. 'She's very big in Bombay Bollywood films. Enormous, in fact. They love her — if not quite for the right reason. She's cornered the market in Memsahibs from Hell.' She gave a hiccoughing little laugh. 'Sheer typecasting, of course.'

It figured. 'She'd be good at it,' I said. 'A sort of Katisha in a sari.'

'Exactly. And the beauty of it is that she doesn't realize it. She thinks she's playing a sympathetic leading role, helping the young lovers to get together, when she's really terrorizing them and keeping them apart.' She gave another semi-hysterical laugh.

'Have another cup of coffee,' I urged.

'Perhaps with a dash of brandy in it?' If Evangeline had left any, that is.

'Thank you, that sounds — No! What am I saying? What are you doing? You're a guest in my house, you shouldn't be waiting on me!'

'I don't mind,' I said truthfully. 'You just sit there and take it easy. It sounds as though you've been having a rough time lately.'

'It's been hell!' Matilda admitted. 'After the dog died, Cecile refused to go near the theatre. I've had to rehearse with her understudy — who's about twenty-six and piles on so much make-up trying to look Cecile's age that she can hardly hold her head up. It threw everything out of balance — as though Teddy weren't bad enough. And Cecile stayed locked up in her room here with that dog's body howling her head off!'

'I suppose that's understandable.' I found myself defending Cecile. 'She and Fleur were together for about twenty years. Most marriages don't last that long.'

'Hers certainly didn't. Nor did my father's. It may be understandable, but it was very unprofessional!' Matilda took a deep breath and added regretfully, 'If only my father had lived a few more years, he'd have divorced Soroya, too, and I wouldn't have been left with this problem.'

'Mmm . . .' I wasn't going to go into that. The gossip I remembered hearing about the late Mr Jordan led me to suspect that, if he'd divorced Soroya, it would only have been to marry a teenage lapdancer.

Where was Evangeline? Where was Eddie? Where, even, was Dame Cecile? I cast around unhappily for a way to change the subject. When the good guys got this beleaguered in a film, it was the cue for the U.S. Cavalry to appear on the horizon, riding to the rescue. Where were they?

I became aware of movement at the doorway, but at floor level. It was none of the above, but any distraction was welcome. Especially this one.

'Cho-Cho-San!' I cheered. 'You got away from her!'

'More than my father ever did.' Matilda was still brooding.

'Was Cho-Cho-San your father's cat?' The explanation for her calling Soroya a liar occurred to me.

'Oh, no!' Matilda laughed bitterly. 'All his attention was taken up by two-legged cats. He had no time for any four-legged ones.'

'You said something about fish earlier.'

Firmly, I pulled the conversation back to the essentials.

'That cupboard over there . . .' Matilda waved in the general direction. 'This establishment doesn't run to cat food, I'm afraid, but you'll find all sorts of seafood there.'

Not quite. There was one tin of tuna and two of salmon — one of them dented. I reached for the tin of tuna — the good old American comfort food.

'I'll split it with you,' I told Cho-Cho-San, realizing anew just how hungry I was. I'd given up on the eggs. In fact, I was beginning to get a fated feeling about them. Who else might show up to claim them if I tried to cook more?

Cho-Cho-San leaned against my ankles in happy agreement as I wrestled with the ringpull, then I remembered I'd used the last of the bread for Soroya's toast. I zeroed in on a breadbox under the cabinet, but found only a very sad-looking wholemeal loaf. Still, if I trimmed off the greenish crusts, the centre was probably safe to eat.

Returning to the fridge, I found I'd used the last of the butter scrambling the eggs. The mayonnaise jar was empty, the cream cheese stood in a puddle of liquid while the top of the cheese was parched and cracked and shrouded in dark blue mould. The chutney was a dark solidified lump at the bottom of the jar and something whose stained and sticky label proclaimed it to be some sort of relish looked so sinister that I didn't bother to open it.

'How long have you been without a housekeeper?' I asked, dribbling a bit of oil from the tuna across the stale bread.

'Oh . . . two or three weeks. Perhaps longer. I've lost track. We've been so busy rehearsing . . . and then we eat out afterwards. I only got round to interviewing a new one a couple of days ago. Why?'

'Just wondering . . .' Matilda was obviously akin to Evangeline: so long as there was a restaurant open, the kitchen held no interest for her.

'That reminds me . . .' Matilda's brow wrinkled. 'Where is Mrs Temple? She was supposed to start work this morning.'

Poor Matilda. Life was just one problem after another for her. Opening night looming, an unwanted stepmother who had moved in, a housekeeper who had decamped without ever having worked for a day — and it couldn't have been much fun to have Dame Cecile stalking around playing the tragedienne since the demise of Fleur-de-Lys.

My own problems paled into insignificance. Actually — fingers crossed — I didn't have that many problems at the moment.

In fact, if my daughter was going to surprise me with the announcement I hoped for, everything was wonderful.

At my feet, Cho-Cho finished her tuna and curled around my ankles again, purring lyrically. I bent and gathered her into my arms, stroking the silky fur while a feeling of immense well-being settled over me. I tried to share it with Matilda.

'Don't worry, everything will sort itself out. Cecile will carry on with the show. Soroya can't hang around too long, if she has all those commitments in Bollywood. Your new housekeeper is bound to turn up sooner or later, probably she got caught up in some train delay. There's absolutely nothing to worry —'

The slam of the front door and a series of piercing screams halted me in mid-sentence.

'You think so, do you?' Matilda cocked a disbelieving eyebrow at me before standing to face the doorway and whatever new crisis was heading towards us.

The front door slammed again and a loud angry voice rose over the screams. Another slam of the front door —they must be slamming it in each other's faces — was followed by a sudden ominous silence.

It appeared that lunch had not gone well. Perhaps I hadn't made such a bad choice after all.

'I have a raging headache!' Evangeline tottered into the room and slumped into the chair Matilda had just vacated.

'I've got indigestion,' Eddie complained, leaning against the wall.

'The pizza parlour was your idea!' Evangeline snapped.

'Yeah, well, sorry about that. I thought she might not make a scene in a place like that. It being out of 'er depth, sort of.'

'Hah!' Evangeline spat bitterly. 'Hah!'

Matilda and I stood watching the doorway. It was like waiting for the other shoe to drop.

'Perhaps she's gone straight up to her room?' I suggested hopefully. Matilda shook her head. It was too much to hope for.

It certainly was. It was just the calm before the storm. I remembered the mirror in the front hall and realized that Dame Cecile had merely paused to check her hair and make-up and, possibly, adjust her expression, before returning to the fray — and fresh victims.

'Get that beast out of my sight!' She appeared in the doorway, attempting to skewer me with a laser-like glare. 'You traitor!'

'Traitor? Me?' I clutched Cho-Cho-San to me protectively, aware that Evangeline and Eddie were relaxing slightly now that Dame Cecile's wrath was turned elsewhere.

'You!' Dame Cecile advanced slowly, one finger pointing in accusation. 'You! Deserting my poor Fleur for that — that —' Cho-Cho-San stretched out her neck and sniffed at the pointing finger, then tried to rub against it. Dame Cecile snatched it away as though it had been burned.

'You!' She backed a few paces. 'I shall never forgive you!'

It was a shame she didn't extend the edict to include never speaking to me again.

'Trixie was right.' Unusually, Evangeline weighed in on my side. 'The cat is alive. There was nothing anyone could do for Fleur. The living must come first.'

Eddie began shaking his head frantically and making shooshing gestures. Abruptly, I remembered that Fleur's was not the only corpse we had left behind in the blazing shop.

'What's going on here?' Matilda was no fool. 'Where *did* you get that cat? She lives on the other side of town.'

'She does? Then who — ?'

'Get that wretched beast out of my sight!' Dame Cecile was off again.

'Perhaps it would be as well to take her into another room,' Matilda murmured. 'At least, until Cecile calms down a bit.'

'I heard that!' Dame Cecile trumpeted. 'And I am perfectly calm!'

'Of course you are.' Evangeline did a *Get out of here!* jerk of her head towards the door and I was glad to slide away.

'Strewth!' Eddie had followed me from the room. 'And I thought you two were the bleedin' limit!'

'Don't be rude. You know we're pussycats.'

'The only pussycat around here is this one.' He held out his hand to Cho-Cho, who sniffed it thoroughly and approved. She rubbed her head against it. 'Pretty little thing, nice nature. What was she doing in that place?'

'Waiting to be stuffed.'

'Never!' Eddie paled. 'But she isn't dead.'

'Exactly.'

'But . . .' Eddie went from pale to green. 'You don't mean . . .'

'There was an empty display case waiting for her. And the instructions for mounting were attached to her cage.' I felt a trifle better at having someone to confide in, even though Eddie was looking worse with every word as the full implications sank in.

'Who'd do a thing like that?'

'Presumably Mr Stuff Yours — if the money was right.'

'Then I 'ope 'e was the geezer I found with 'is 'ead bashed in. 'E 'ad it coming to 'im!'

I nodded agreement. Eddie began scratching Cho-Cho's ears and making little soothing sounds. ' 'Ow could anybody want to 'urt you, sweet'eart?'

'Maybe he didn't want to.' It was a good question and a possible answer presented itself. 'Maybe he refused to do it — and that was why he was killed.'

'Then there's a madman runnin' loose!' Eddie looked around uneasily. 'Somebody's dead crazy!'

'That's very possible.' Surely no normal person could be so cold-hearted and vicious. What twisted mind would want to consign an innocent cat to such a horrible fate? Could it be someone who hated her owner, who wanted revenge? *'Deliver to:'* had been the last line below the mounting instructions, the name and address had been torn away.

Deliver to Soroya Jordan? I could understand someone hating her that much, but did she care enough about Cho-Cho to be properly devastated by such a delivery? She seemed to spend most of her time in Bollywood, leaving the cat behind. In whose care? Anyway, Matilda said that she had lied about the cat being hers. Presumably, there was someone with a greater claim to Cho-Cho-San, someone who cared more about her.

I needed to have a talk with Matilda. Privately. The low murmur of voices from the kitchen told me there was no hope of that right now.

'Gone a bit quiet out there.' Eddie looked in that direction. 'Think you might roust out your chum? We ought to be getting back to civilization.'

'That's not a bad idea.' I started forward, then turned back. 'Here, hold Cho-Cho for me. I don't want to start Dame Cecile off again.'

'That's it, you come to your Uncle Eddie,' he crooned, as Cho-Cho settled trustingly in his arms. 'Don't you worry about a thing. We'll see you right.'

There was a sudden eruption of hysterics from the kitchen and I nearly collided in the doorway with Matilda, who was trying to escape just as I was trying to enter.

'You're still here!' she gasped. 'That cat's

still here! Get it out of here before Cecile sees it again!'

'But . . . Soroya will be looking for —'

'Soroya doesn't have to go onstage with Cecile next week!' She caught me by the shoulders and pushed me back. 'I'll take care of Soroya — you hold on to the cat until after the opening.'

I tried to hide my delight. 'I suppose we could take her back to London with us . . .'

Chapter Five

We slept late in the morning. At least, I did. I wasn't sure about Cho-Cho's usual sleeping habits. She had begun the night stretched out at my feet but, when I awoke, I found her curled in the crook of my arm. She chirruped a happy 'Good morning' as I opened my eyes.

'Ah, well,' I said. 'Let's go see what we can find for breakfast.'

We found Evangeline and Nigel huddled together like conspirators at the kitchen table. They leapt apart guiltily when they realized I was in the doorway.

'Ah!' Nigel said. 'Ah! There you are!' Quite as though he had been looking for me, although I got the distinct impression that I was the last person in the world he really wanted to see. He eyed me warily as I advanced into the room.

But not half as warily as Cho-Cho-San eyed him. She sank lower to the floor and crept up on him, sniffing at his shoes and looking increasingly suspicious and puzzled. She moved a bit closer and investigated his trouser cuffs.

'What's that?' Nigel became aware of her and swung his legs out of range.

'Trixie has rescued a cat!' Evangeline proclaimed in martyred tones. 'But we can't keep it here,' she added nastily. 'We're just putting up with it — I mean, putting it up — for a couple of days.'

'Ah!' Nigel regarded Cho-Cho uneasily. 'It doesn't need walking, does it?' He had not appreciated his tours of duty with an Irish wolfhound.

'Cats can take care of themselves,' I reassured him, shooting Evangeline a dirty look. 'She won't be any trouble at all.' I made a mental note to get to a pet shop that afternoon and pick up a litter tray and a few accessories. A toy or two might not go amiss.

Cho-Cho took a final sniff at Nigel's socks and strolled away to inspect the kitchen. I went to see what I could find in the fridge to feed her. As I thought, there was plenty.

I have always prided myself on maintaining a well-stocked fridge. Compared to Matilda Jordan's, it was a cornucopia of riches. I hoped her new housekeeper would turn up and take over soon. I'd never met anyone more in need of a housekeeper.

I wrenched a few chunks of chicken off

the carcass of yesterday's supper and took a raspberry Danish from the freezer compartment for myself.

I was crossing to zap it in the microwave when, out of the corner of my eye, I caught a surreptitious movement at the table. I turned to see Evangeline slide a small oblong piece of paper towards Nigel.

A cheque-sized piece of paper.

He palmed it expertly and transferred it to an inside pocket.

Well, if she was fool enough to have any financial dealings with Nigel, it was her funeral.

I immediately wished I hadn't had that thought. It brought back the memory of the taxidermist's shop that had turned into a funeral pyre — for man and beasts.

On the way back to London yesterday, I had tried tactfully to persuade Eddie that it was his civic duty to tell the police that there had been a dead body in the back of the shop. Even if he had to relay the information via another anonymous phone call.

Shades of de Mille, Preminger, Selznick and Zanuck — the way that man carried on! I certainly won't make a suggestion like that again. For a nasty moment, I'd thought he was going to turn us out of the cab and make us walk back to London.

We had placated him and assured him that we had no intention of telling the police anything ourselves. How could we? We hadn't seen the body. Eddie was the only eyewitness who could describe it — and he didn't want to get involved. I couldn't really say that I blamed him.

'Ah, well!' Nigel pushed back his chair as I set the saucer of chicken on the floor for an eager Cho-Cho and retrieved my now thawed raspberry Danish from the microwave. 'Mustn't keep you any longer. Know you have things to do. I'll be on my way, see myself out.' He left at a brisk trot and we heard the front door slam behind him.

I poured myself a cup of coffee and took the chair he had just vacated.

'Don't look at me in that tone of voice,' Evangeline said. 'I know what I'm doing.'

'Hmmm . . .'

Cho-Cho had gulped down her chicken already — can cats get indigestion? — and sauntered back to me hopefully.

'Nice kitty . . .' Ever one to latch on to a distraction when she was in trouble, Evangeline leaned over to stroke her.

Cho-Cho accepted the caress, but was far more interested in the plastic carrier bag with the exclusive logo resting beside Evangeline's chair. She pawed at it delicately and it toppled over. She promptly wriggled into it.

'Here, now, stop that! What are you doing?' Evangeline snatched at the disappearing cat. 'Come out of there!'

The bag shimmied and rocked, feathers suddenly flew out of the opening.

'Don't ruin it!' Evangeline caught the bottom of the squirming bag and upended it, tumbling out the cat entangled in a nest of feathers.

Cho-Cho shook herself and pranced away, trailing a long banner of feathers on either side of her, clearly delighted with the plaything she had discovered.

As well she might be. I hadn't seen an ostrich feather boa like that since *Darling of the Bowery.*

'Where on earth did you get that?' I gasped.

'Dear Nigel brought it for me. He says it's the latest thing.'

'Perhaps it is . . .' We both watched as Cho-Cho rolled over on her back and kicked out wildly at the boa, sending multicoloured fronds flying through the air. 'But do you think it's really you?'

'Possibly not,' she admitted. 'It looks far more like her. And —' a crafty expression brightened her face — 'if she tears it to pieces, it won't be my fault if I can't wear it when Nigel takes me out to dinner.'

'How true!' I caught up one end of the long boa and trailed it enticingly across Cho-Cho's nose. She sneezed, then arched and twisted, doing a manic somersault to land on her feet and attack this new menace. A storm of feathers eddied upwards.

'Good girl! Catch it! Kill it!' Evangeline egged her on. She took the other end of the boa and looped it around Cho-Cho's powderpuff of a tail. Cho-Cho twisted madly to capture it.

Evangeline gave a sudden schoolgirl giggle and I found myself matching it. Cho-Cho's antics were irresistible. We stood in a snowstorm of feathers, giggling wildly, egging the cat on to ever wilder excesses. I swear Cho-Cho was giggling, too. We were all having a wonderful time.

The sudden peal of the doorbell stopped us all dead in our tracks. We looked at each other in silent agreement: we weren't expecting company.

'Perhaps Nigel forgot something?' I looked guiltily at the carpet of feathers. Where was the broom?

'I hope he doesn't want his boa back!' A stray giggle escaped Evangeline.

'Yoo-hoo . . . Mother . . .' Martha yo-delled through the letter slot in the door. 'It's me. Are you there?'

'I'll get it!' I rushed down the hallway as Evangeline slumped back in her chair. Cho-Cho shook herself, sat down and began to wash her face, quite as though all the surrounding mess and the half-denuded boa had nothing to do with her.

Martha wasn't alone. Startled, I stepped back a pace. I had never seen the woman with her before.

'Mother —' Martha kissed me absently, beaming, lost in some dream of her own. 'Mother, I can tell you now. It's happened! The contracts are all signed!'

'Darling, I'm so happy for you . . .' Wait a minute — what had she said? Wasn't this going to be what I had been hoping to hear? 'What do you mean — contracts?'

'For the book, Mother.' Martha was ab-solutely glowing, but for the wrong reason. 'The cookbook I'm going to do.'

'You mean you're not — I'm not going to be a —' I managed to stop short of the fatal words. Fortunately, Martha did not notice.

'And this is Jocasta Purley — from the publishers. She's going to help me with it.'

'I'm so delighted to meet you, Ms

Dolan.' The young woman stepped forward and grasped my hand. 'I've enjoyed so many of your films — on television, of course.'

'Thank you.' I freed my hand with the firm conviction that we were not about to become the best of friends, Martha notwithstanding. 'We're in the kitchen, come and have some coffee.'

Martha led the way and I lingered to make sure the door was properly closed, sometimes the latch sticks. When I reached the kitchen, Jocasta was regaling Evangeline with the information that she truly adored all those really, really old films on TV and how Evangeline's early performances never failed to enthral her. I took a quick look to make sure that the sharpest knife on the table was the butter knife and began a fresh pot of coffee.

'Sit down, Jocasta,' Martha tried to signal her nervously. 'Would you like a Danish or a muffin?' But there was no stopping the woman.

'Perhaps you'll appreciate what a thrill this is for me, Miss Sinclair,' she gushed on, 'if I tell you that my grandmother was one of your greatest fans. She used to tell me bedtime stories made up from your films — well, censored, of course. And she did a terrific imitation of you. Why, you're positively a tradition in our family!'

I snatched away the pepper pot just as Evangeline's fingers closed around it.

'Have you seen the view?' Martha burbled, getting a firm grip on Jocasta's arm and pulling her along. 'Come into the drawing room — it's quite sensational from there.'

'Try to be polite.' I blocked Evangeline's path as Martha led Jocasta away. 'A fan is a fan — especially if it runs in the family. And stop grinding your teeth like that — you'll break your caps and we don't have a dentist in this country.'

Evangeline's nostrils flared as she took several deep breaths. 'Get that woman out of here before I kill her!'

'Take it easy,' I soothed. 'She's just a bit overcome — you know how it goes. Now that she's made her little speech, she'll settle down.' Martha would see to that.

I hadn't realized Cho-Cho-San had slipped out of sight until she reappeared, looking quite pleased with herself. It's a clever cat who knows when it's wise to disappear. But, if she was so clever, how had she wound up in a taxidermist's shop? Perhaps because she had trusted the wrong person?

'Where have you been?' I asked.

'Wherever it was, she can go right back!' Evangeline, having lost one battle, rushed into another. 'You can't keep her here.'

'She's going back to her owner in a couple of days.' Or to one of them. She seemed to have two claimants, at least. I would have to pin Matilda down.

'Oh, how perfect! I always feel that a place isn't a real home without a cat!' Jocasta was back. The glories of the riverscape were obviously no match for the attraction of a Family Tradition in the kitchen. 'And I might have known *you'd* have an exotic cat.' She gazed at Evangeline adoringly.

Evangeline smiled stiffly, but I noticed that she stopped shifting her legs and allowed Cho-Cho to encircle her ankles.

'And this kitchen! It's fantastic!' Even though she was a cookery expert and presumably accustomed to all sorts of kitchens, Jocasta seemed awe-stricken. 'I've never seen anything like it! It's so — so — ultra-modern!'

'Twenty-second century, at least,' I agreed, resisting the temptation to challenge her to identify the built-in oven. It had taken me two days and I was living here.

'I'm sure you must make the most wonderful dishes here,' Jocasta continued swiftly, as though subliminally aware of a certain chill in the atmosphere. 'Martha told me you were wonderful cooks.'

I doubted that Martha had included Evangeline in her endorsement, but smiled blandly. Evangeline preened herself, ready to accept any accolade, however unlikely.

Still gazing at Evangeline with sickening adoration, Jocasta opened her mouth again, but I got in first.

'Darling,' I said to Martha, 'you haven't told me yet what this is all about. How did you get into this? What kind of cookbook are you doing? Is there a theme to it?'

'How clever of you, Mother. Of course there is. There has to be these days, doesn't there? We were talking about the idea at the Lady Lemmings' meeting when we were considering different ways of earning money. You know how they're always trying to raise funds for their charitable works.'

I nodded. The Lady Lemmings were a long-standing show business organization comprising the distaff side of the profession. It began with the wives, whose ranks had soon been swollen by working or resting actresses, designers, assistant stage managers, dressers and anyone else on the female side of the business. Their charities were many; their disagreements legendary. As the wife of one of the West End's most distinguished producers, Martha had been co-opted into their ranks before the petals of her bridal bouquet had had time to wilt. When the present incumbent had been beaten away from the star position in the organization, Martha was a certainty to be voted into that position — unless (God forbid!) something dire had happened to Hugh in the meantime.

'We decided on a cookbook with everyone from stars to beginners providing their favourite recipes —' She ignored Evangeline's snort and went on. 'Most of the members voted for smaller portion recipes, for one or two people. Or one person with something left over for a snack the next day. They pointed out that so many of the theatrical lodgings of their early days — where the landlady supplied breakfast and supper — had disappeared and now been replaced by hotel rooms or self-service apartments, there should be a good market for that —'

'We're calling it *One for the Road*,' Jocasta cut in smoothly. 'And all proceeds will go to the Lady Lemmings for their charities.'

'I see.' I made a mental bet that those

77

proceeds didn't include Jocasta's fees and expenses. 'It sounds really wonderful, darling.' Now I was the one ignoring Evangeline's snort.

'And I'm sure —' Jocasta was looking at Evangeline again — 'you'll both have some wonderful contributions to make.'

'I'll certainly think about it.' I would, if only for Martha's sake. 'I just wish all my recipes weren't on the other side of the Atlantic.'

'Oh, it isn't just recipes we want,' Jocasta said quickly. 'We want useful tips, short cuts, all the sorts of things to make life easier for actors on tour who have to fend for themselves, perhaps late at night in the provinces, after the last show, when the pubs are closed and they can't face one more curry house or Chinese takeaway — even if any were still open.'

A wave of nostalgia swept over me as I remembered my early days in New York, one of the struggling chorus kids they called 'gypsies', where, no matter how many others we shared a cold water walk-up apartment with, we were still outnumbered at least fifty-to-one by the cockroaches. Back when every penny counted and the big worry about weight was not keeping it down, but scraping together enough calories to sustain us through the long and punishing dance routines when we were lucky enough to get a place in the chorus. Sometimes it was hard to realize that, give or take a few variations, the new kids coming along today were faced with the same problems.

'I thought I'd call the first chapter "The Collapsible Cupboard",' Martha said. 'You know, giving a list of lots of spices and dried herbs that come in — or can be decanted into — little envelopes and add so much pep to basic meals. And then there are the packet soups, like onion, that can be used as a base for more ambitious dishes.'

'And don't forget all the little single portion packs you can pick up in cafeterias,' I prompted, seldom in those days having left such an establishment without unused sugar packets and anything else out on free display crammed into my pockets. 'All those sachets of mustard, mayonnaise, Worcestershire sauce, vinegar, tartare sauce — oh! and tomato ketchup, lots and lots of ketchup. How I remember tomato ketchup soup!' I sighed reminiscently, then became aware of Jocasta eyeing me coldly.

'Actually,' she said, ice dripping from her tones, 'we were planning something rather more upmarket than that!'

'Beyond the Pot Noodle . . .' Evangeline said dreamily.

'That's wonderful!' Jocasta whirled to face her, all enthusiasm now. 'Martha, did you hear that? We have a title for another chapter. If you don't mind, that is?' She gave Evangeline a servile smile.

'Of course you may use it,' Evangeline said graciously. 'I'm always happy to help a good cause. In fact, as for tips . . .' She hesitated. 'No, it's probably silly . . .'

'Oh, no, no!' Jocasta clasped her hands together earnestly. 'We'd love to hear it!'

Martha and I exchanged glances. Evangeline was doing well to find her way into a kitchen, never mind have any tips for doing anything once she was there. Apart from eating everything that someone else had cooked, of course.

'It's just one of my little ways . . .' Evangeline paused for the encouragement which was immediately forthcoming.

'Yes?' Jocasta breathed, leaning forward so as not to miss a syllable of the great revelation. 'Yes . . . ?'

'I don't know of anyone else who does it. I've never seen it mentioned in any cookbook . . .'

'Yes? Yes?'

'But, whenever I'm going to do any cooking, I always wash my hands with oatmeal soap.'

Well, that explained why I'd never seen any oatmeal soap in the house.

'Oh, yes!' Jocasta was buying it unreservedly. 'Oh, I knew I could depend on you for real gourmet secrets! What a splendid idea!'

Martha closed her eyes and leaned back in her chair. I felt a little dizzy myself.

'Oh, please, don't stop there!' Jocasta produced a small notebook from her handbag and began scribbling rapidly. 'Go on. What other wonderful tips have you?'

'Oh, I don't know . . .' Evangeline demurred, trying to look modest, while her eyes shifted uneasily. She'd shot her bolt and she knew it and she knew I knew it. 'I'll have to think.'

'Actually —' Martha deflected Jocasta's attention — 'Mother is the real cook around here. She'll have dozens of good tips.'

'One I've found really useful —' I picked up on my cue — 'is knowing that in almost all savoury and spicy dishes, curries and the like, when the recipe calls for an apple, you can substitute a carrot instead. You're often more likely to have carrots around than apples.'

'Mmm, yes.' Jocasta entered the note unenthusiastically. It obviously wasn't gourmet and glamorous enough for her. I got the feeling I was being downmarket again. Perhaps I should have suggested kiwi fruit.

'And you . . . ?' She turned back to Evangeline expectantly, hoping for more priceless words of wisdom.

'My head . . .' Evangeline brushed a hand across her forehead and swayed weakly. 'I'm sorry . . .' She rose, still swaying. 'I'm so afraid I have one of my headaches coming on. I must go and lie down.'

A cellphone burbled suddenly, and Evangeline nearly gave the game away by the alacrity with which she dived for a handbag she had forgotten she'd left in her room.

'Hello? Oh, yes, darling.' It was Martha's phone. 'Yes, yes, I see. Of course, right away. . . . Yes, I'll tell them.' She looked up. 'Hugh sends his love.'

'And ours to him,' I responded. Evangeline snorted.

'I'm sorry, but we'll have to leave now.' Martha turned to Jocasta. 'My husband has had overseas friends arrive unexpectedly. We'll have to entertain them.' She stood and pecked at my cheek. 'I'll get back to you later on this.'

'Don't forget, we'll be going down to Brighton for Dame Cecile's opening,' I reminded her. 'We'll be there overnight. Matilda has invited us to stay with her.'

'Dame Cecile Savoy and Matilda Jordan?' Jocasta was revitalized. 'They go back to the great days of touring companies and theatrical digs. Oh, I'll bet they'd have some marvellous recipes for the book!'

'Mmm.' I thought of Matilda's neglected fridge and declined to commit myself. Not so Evangeline.

'Yes, indeed!' She paused in the doorway and turned back to Jocasta with the radiant smile she displays when selling someone down the river.

'Oh, you'll find Dame Cecile a positive gold mine of culinary wisdom!'

Chapter Six

'Look at that!' It wasn't long after they had left when Eddie arrived. 'Look at that!' He stormed past me as I opened the door and rushed into the drawing room, flinging down a newspaper on to the coffee table in front of the sofa where Evangeline was lounging. 'Just look at that!'

'Oh?' Evangeline looked at the copy of the *Argus* he had hurled on to the table. 'Have you been down to Brighton again?'

'No — and I'm not going again! Will you look at that!'

She wouldn't. Evangeline had gone into one of her maddening moods. 'I don't understand. What are you doing with the Brighton paper then? Did someone leave it in your cab?'

'I bought it at London Bridge station.' Eddie took a deep breath and forestalled her next question. 'You can buy it at Victoria station late afternoons, too. Same as you can buy the out-of-town newspapers at any station where you catch the train to that place. Commuters like it that way. They can read the local paper on their way 'ome and be up to speed on what's 'appening in their town by the time they get there.'

'If they like their town that much, why don't they stay in it?'

'Because the best-paying jobs are in London! Now will you — ?'

'Oh, no!' While they were bickering, I had taken possession of the paper. No wonder Eddie was so upset. There it was — in front page headlines: MAN DEAD IN ARSON ATTACK. POLICE SEARCH FOR SUSPECTS SEEN FLEEING BLAZE.

'What is it?' Now that I had the paper, Evangeline wanted it. She wrenched it away from me, leaving me with a strip of white margin and a few fragmented bits of print.

'Someone must have seen us!' How could we have imagined otherwise? That narrow cul-de-sac, with all the ramshackle eighteenth-century houses leaning together higgledy-piggledy and doubtless crammed with low-rent tenants, either retired or unemployed, with plenty of time on their hands to mind everybody else's business. The first hint of smoke drifting through the cracks of those tinderbox dwellings would have brought anxious faces to windows, checking that the danger was outside and not within.

'Good job no one recognized you. Unless . . .' Eddie's brow furrowed. 'Unless they did recognize you and the cops are keeping it up their sleeves so you can be identified when you're caught.'

'You were there, too!' All those *yous* were clearly getting on Evangeline's nerves.

'That's why I'm not going back there again. And, if you're smart, you won't, either.'

'We've promised Cecile we'll attend the opening.' Evangeline drew herself up proudly, quite as though she had never broken a promise in her life. 'We can't let her down.'

And I could do with less of the *we* stuff. I'd never met Dame Cecile before in my life — not until Evangeline introduced her to me a few months ago. She was Evangeline's old friend.

'I don't know,' I said. 'Eddie has a point.'

'Too bloody right, I 'ave!' At his feet, Cho-Cho-San gave a friendly chirrup and rubbed against his ankles. He looked down and his expression softened. 'They're nasty people down there. Look what they tried to do to Little Sweet'eart, 'ere.' She nuzzled him contentedly as he picked her up and cuddled her in his arms. 'You want to stay away from bleeders like that!'

Score another point for Eddie. A point I hadn't forgotten. I hadn't decided what I could do about the situation, but I did know that I was reluctant to take her back to Brighton where she might be in danger again.

'Out of the question!' Evangeline set her jaw stubbornly. 'We're going. And, if you're not willing to take us, we'll hire another cab!'

' 'Ere now, you needn't be like that!' Eddie hated to miss anything. 'Let me 'ave a think and maybe we can sort something out. I've got a cousin —'

'We'll all have another think.' I gave Eddie a *Leave it to me* nod. I had a few more days to work on Evangeline and to bring her around to our way of thinking.

At least, I thought I had.

I spent the rest of the day in a Fool's Paradise. Before he left, Eddie drove us over to the supermarket to pick up supplies and back again. Evangeline sniffed when she saw me putting kitty litter and cat food into my trolley, but I noticed that she absently slipped a catnip mouse into her own basket.

After Eddie had dumped all the shopping bags on the kitchen table and departed, I began unpacking them. With Martha's new project in mind, I had picked up an assortment of sauces and spices. I'd try to remember some of the recipes I'd relied on in my early solo days.

To begin with, I tossed a few pepper-corns and a clove of garlic into the largest saucepan, then unwrapped the pair of chicken legs, put them into the pan and filled it with cold water before covering it and putting it on the stove to boil.

'Hmmph!' Evangeline disdained my ef-forts. 'I distinctly remember that when my mother made chicken soup she boiled up the whole leftover carcass.'

'So did mine — and I'll never forget the thrill when I discovered you didn't need to eat cold chicken for a week before you got to make soup. It was like that Charles Lamb story when the people discovered that they didn't have to burn the house down to make roast pork.'

'I know that story.' Evangeline grinned reminiscently. 'They burned down most of the village before they finally got the hang of it and invented the barbecue.'

'And I ate a lot of weak soup before I found the best base was two whole legs — thigh and drumstick.' I had been putting the shopping away while we talked, now I chopped an onion and carrot, ready to tip into the pot at the half-hour mark. Another half-hour after that, and I'd take the legs out, one at a time, and skin and bone them before dicing the meat and returning it to the pot which was still simmering on the stove. Then just ladle it out and eat.

Through it all, Cho-Cho-San frolicked at my feet, trilling with excitement. She tried to catch the shreds as I scraped the carrots and sniffed blissfully at the chicken scent beginning to permeate the air. It was a learning experience for her: food did not just come out of little round tins. It told me something else about her: she was not accustomed to food preparation and cooking. Perhaps she had belonged to a man — or, remembering Matilda's fridge, a woman with no great interest in food. From the size of her, one would not put Soroya into that category, but I had the feeling that her interest in food did not extend beyond the eating of it. Someone else could do the work involved.

The closing day merged almost imperceptibly into an evening of rare domestic tranquillity. The saucepan produced two bowls of soup each, plus one for Cho-Cho. I do like to see my cooking appreciated. Cho-Cho ate everything but a lone peppercorn that had found its way into her bowl. Evangeline crunched her peppercorns with zest. I'd purchased ready-made profiteroles for us and shared a generous dollop of cream with Cho-Cho.

'The Pick of the Day,' Evangeline announced, scanning the evening paper's TV listings, 'is *Fools Rush In*. It seems to be Matilda Jordan's first film — starring her father, Gervaise, in his prime.'

'We can't miss that,' I agreed. We settled on the sofa in front of the TV, Cho-Cho curled up between us, purring happily, and we all watched the film.

Matilda had been so young, so beautiful, so vulnerable — and yet there was an intriguing hint of world-weariness about her that caught at her audience. Especially when she looked at her father and his leading lady.

'That was Gervaise's third wife, I believe,' Evangeline said. 'Or possibly, his fourth. There were very messy divorce cases on both sides, as I recall. But then, there usually were.'

Matilda had come by her world-weariness honestly. Gervaise was the sort who would age any woman rapidly.

But, oh, that woman — any woman except his daughter — might have had a wonderful time. At first.

No doubt about it, Gervaise Jordan had it all: the lean lithe body, the charm, the grace, the smothering intensity as he concentrated every fibre of his being upon his leading lady. You could understand why shopgirls had swooned in the aisles, while their less prepossessing escorts ground their teeth. And there couldn't have been many men who were more prepossessing than Gervaise.

Then the scene shifted and he was in top hat and tails, walking along the river promenade with his lady. No doubt about it, Gervaise Jordan had been the matinée idol's Matinée Idol.

'Oh,' I sighed, as the violins struck up. 'They don't make them like that any more.'

'Just as well,' Evangeline said. 'Look at that roving eye. He can't keep it still for a moment.'

Sure enough, Gervaise's attention had strayed over his co-star's shoulder to check out some little extra who was selling flowers, in the artless way they did in old films, nowhere near any place where she might find a steady flow of customers. She was just standing obligingly on the path waiting for one pair of starry-eyed lovers. She was never going to make a living in the real world.

Rather, her character wasn't. She, as I seemed to recall, had caught the producer's eye, as well as Gervaise's, and more fruitfully.

'Didn't she wind up as — ?'

'A star, a Lady and matriarch of a theatrical dynasty,' Evangeline supplied. 'Not necessarily in that order.'

'Oh, look!' I pointed to a corner of the screen. 'There he goes again! I saw him wink at the girl walking the dog. I'm sure that wasn't in the script.'

'Randy old bastard.' Evangeline frowned. 'Easily discouraged, though. He even tried to get funny with me once — and I let him have it with the seltzer bottle. He was no trouble after that.'

'A faceful of seltzer water would discourage any man,' I agreed.

'Who said anything about his face? I aimed it where he'd notice it most — and so would everyone else. He looked as though he'd had an embarrassing accident. He had to rush away and change before anyone saw him. He kept his distance after that — he was afraid of what I might do for an encore.'

'You could almost feel sorry for him,' I laughed.

'No need. He took off shortly after that on a Triumphal Tour of the Antipodes where, rumour had it, he cut a wider swathe among the local female talent than even the late dear Duke of Windsor. He did so well he returned several times and did a lot of entertaining the troops in that region during the war and afterwards. I'll wager he didn't entertain them half so much as he entertained himself with the girls they left behind them.'

' 'Twas ever thus,' I sighed. Star-struck females were ripe for the plucking by an unscrupulous male — and not necessarily the star. Anyone in the entourage would do, if they thought it would get them closer to their goal.

'Oh, look . . .' An organ grinder had strolled into the scene, playing the featured theme music. 'I haven't seen him in years. I know his face, now what was his name . . . ?'

Half the fun of these old movies is spotting old friends, adversaries and acquaintances, all viewed now with the luxury of hindsight. Now we knew the anecdotes, scandals, stories and ultimate fates trailing in their wake, things we had not suspected at the time.

We had a wonderful evening dissecting everyone and everything. Sometimes we even watched the screen. It was the most satisfying and peaceful evening we had enjoyed in weeks.

Which was just as well. Late the next morning, all hell broke loose.

Chapter Seven

We were having a leisurely brunch when Evangeline's mobile phone began ringing. Of course, she'd left it in her bedroom and had to go and find it.

'*Wha-a-t?*' The modified shriek brought me to my feet, sending Cho-Cho tumbling to the floor. We both dashed in the direction of the incoherent shrieks.

'Evangeline, what is it? What's the matter?'

'Don't worry, Eddie,' she said into the phone. 'We'll help you. We'll get you out of this.'

'What is it? What's happened?'

'What do you mean —' her face froze — 'we've done enough?'

'Let me talk to him.' I wrestled the phone from her.

'I told them I'd been with you all day,' Eddie's plaintive voice was saying. 'Evangeline Sinclair, Trixie Dolan and Dame Cecile Savoy. "Just ask them," I said, "they're my alibi." And they said, "Pull the other one, there's bells on it." '

'Alibi? What do you mean, alibi?

Eddie, what's going on?'

'Ron!' Evangeline abandoned her attempt to get the phone back. 'Ron Heyhoe! Where's my address book? Ron will know what to do. He'll have friends down there —'

'Down where? Eddie, where are you?'

'Brighton,' Eddie said lugubriously. 'Bloody Brighton.'

'Brighton? What are you doing there? You told us yesterday you never wanted to go there again.'

'I didn't,' he said. 'But they came and got me.'

'Got you? Eddie —'

'Got it!' Evangeline surfaced from the depths of a drawer, waving her address book triumphantly. 'Now . . .' she began riffling the pages. 'Ron . . . Heyhoe, Ron, Superintendent.'

'Some git took my licence number,' Eddie said. 'Gave it to the coppers, didn't 'e? So, 'ere I am, under arr— No, no, I'm not finished. Let me talk. I —' The line went dead.

'Eddie!' I pushed buttons wildly, trying to get him back, but nothing happened.

'Ah, here it is!' Evangeline dived for the regular telephone and began stabbing numbers.

'Wait for me!' I abandoned the attempt to reach Eddie and rushed to the extension. I wasn't going to miss this.

'Superintendent Heyhoe, please. It's an emergency . . . Certainly, this is Evangeline Sinclair.'

I picked up the extension in time to hear an ominous silence. Then a click and a heavy sigh announced that we had been put through.

'Ron? Superintendent Heyhoe? Ron, is that you?'

'Good morning, Miss Sinclair. What's the problem?' His doom-laden tone expected the worst — and he was going to get it.

'Now, Ron, you promised you were going to call me Evangeline, remember?' That was her idea of softening him up.

'What do you want . . . Evangeline?' He wasn't buying it.

'I was just thinking . . . it's been such a long time since we've seen each other. Why don't we get together for a drink? Soon.'

'Evangeline, I have a drug-related shooting, six mobile phone muggings, two burglaries and a missing child on my hands right now. If that's all you have on your mind, perhaps we could discuss it at a later time.'

'Oh! . . . Well, there *is* a teensy-weensy little

problem . . . I'm afraid it's rather urgent.'

'*How* teensy-weensy? *How* urgent? What have you done now?'

'It isn't us. It's our friend, Eddie. You know, the taxi driver.'

'Sorry.' He didn't sound it, he sounded relieved. 'I can't do anything about parking tickets or traffic violations.'

'Oh, it's nothing like that! I wouldn't dream of bothering you about little things like that.'

'No?' He paused for thought, then asked uneasily: 'What did you mean by urgent?'

'Umm . . . well . . . I'm afraid Eddie has been arrested.'

'Why?'

'It's all a terrible mistake. Some busy-body saw his taxi — we hired him to take us down to Brighton for the day — and reported him. He had nothing to do with what happened. None of us did.'

'If it happened in Brighton, it's way out of my bailiwick.' Again he sounded relieved. 'I can't do anything about it.'

'I know that. I wouldn't expect you to. I was just hoping you knew someone down there who could help us. One of your police colleagues. You all know each other, don't you?'

'I wouldn't say that.' It was clear that he

didn't really want to say anything — except, perhaps, goodbye — but curiosity was getting the better of him. 'What's the charge?'

'Charge?' Evangeline was stalling for time, as though that might make the explanation easier.

'The charge.' It just made Ron more suspicious. 'Contrary to certain assumptions on the part of the public, the police do not just arrest people on a whim. They usually have good cause. What is it?'

'Er, actually, I'm afraid there's more than one,' Evangeline admitted. 'The kidnapping part of it is ridiculous. Cecile will tell you that herself — just as soon as she gets over her snit.'

'Cecile? Savoy? You mean *Dame* Cecile Savoy is involved in this?' he groaned.

'Cecile is the least of it.' I could hold back no longer.

'Thank you, Trixie, I needed that.' His voice was grim. 'Go on, Evangeline. What else?'

'We really just stumbled into it —'

'And stumbled out.' I added moral support.

'Evangeline —' It wasn't appreciated. At least, not by him.

'We had nothing to do with the arson.

The fire had obviously been set and smouldering before we arrived. It just happened to break out while we were there.'

'Kidnapping . . . arson . . .' Ron was bemused.

'It had obviously been set to cover up the murder. Eddie discovered the body in the back room just before the fire exploded.'

I distinctly heard a whimper at the far end of the line.

'Ron . . . ? Ron . . . ?' Evangeline called anxiously. 'Are you still there? You *are* going to help us, aren't you? You must know somebody down there we can turn to?'

There was a long silence.

'Ron . . . ?'

'I'm thinking,' he said. 'I'm trying to decide who I hate enough.'

'Oh, Ron!' Evangeline giggled girlishly with relief. There are moments when even she can tell she may have gone too far. 'You're such a tease!'

'Perhaps Thursby,' he said.

'Not until next Thursday? We need someone now!'

'Not Thursday, Thursby,' he corrected. 'When we were rookies there was a rugby game. We were on opposing sides, of course. He wrecked my knee with a dirty tackle. Put me out of action for months. I still get nasty twinges in bad weather. Yes. Definitely Superintendent Hector Thursby. I owe him one.'

My weekend case was nearly packed when I looked up and into a pair of accusing eyes.

'Cho-Cho! I'd almost forgotten you!' She blinked. That was what she had been afraid of. I was going off and leaving her. But I couldn't leave her here on her own with no one I would trust to look after her properly.

'You'll have to come along with us,' I told her. 'I'm sorry. I know I've promised you that you'd never have to get back in that awful carrier again but —'

'What on earth?' Evangeline appeared in the doorway. 'I thought you were on the phone. What are you doing here talking to yourself?'

'I'm talking to Cho-Cho-San.'

'Same thing.' Evangeline sniffed and regarded the cat coldly. 'What are you going to do with her while we're away?'

'We'll have to take her with us.'

'Nonsense!' Evangeline began, then hesitated. 'On the other hand, that might not be a bad idea. We can watch people's reaction to her. Someone may be very surprised to find she's still alive. Someone who expected her to have perished in that fire.'

'Maybe . . .' I shuddered and tried to pull myself back from thinking about that. 'But we can't be sure that the person who brought Cho-Cho to the shop, the person who killed the man in the back room and the person who set the fire are all one and the same person.'

'Perhaps not, but it's too many coincidences otherwise, wouldn't you say?'

'Possibly.' I hated to admit it, but she could be right. 'Certainly, I'd bet that the killer set the fire, but the person who tried to dispose of Cho-Cho could be someone else entirely.'

'That would mean two cold-blooded merciless people converging on the same shop at the same time. Do you really think that's likely?'

'Why not? The kind of people who go to that kind of shop have to be pretty cold-blooded in the first place.' I threw the last few essentials into my case and zipped it shut.

'The immediate problem,' Evangeline brooded, 'is: what are we going to do for transportation? We relied on Eddie, but he's in jail. You didn't happen to catch the name of his cousin?'

'He didn't throw it.' I picked up the case and followed her into the hall. 'Why don't we just rough it and use public transport? I understand the trains go frequently.'

'Don't be absurd!'

'Evangeline!' I stared aghast at the pile of cases beside the front door and saw what she meant. 'We're not going to Outer Mongolia! Only to Brighton — and it's full of shops and boutiques. If you've forgotten anything, you can just pop out and buy it. You don't need all that luggage!'

I'd once been in a small road company that had barnstormed from Seattle to Paducah with less. And that had included some of the larger chunks of scenery.

'Now . . . who could recommend a good car hire firm?' She paid no attention. As usual. 'Why don't you ring Martha and ask? Perhaps Hugh would volunteer his car.'

'I don't know about that . . .' I hesitated. As though on cue, the phone rang.

'That may be Ron's friend!' Evangeline snatched it up. 'Hello? . . . Oh.' Her face fell, she held the phone out to me. 'It's for you.'

'Mother!' Martha's voice was loud and

distraught. 'Mother — we have an emergency on our hands!'

'The children!' I gasped, my heart sinking. 'What — ?'

'The children are fine. It's the book!'

'Is that all? I mean, I'm sorry, dear. What's gone wrong with the book?'

'There's nothing wrong with the book — except that it may never be finished. It's Jocasta! It's disaster!'

'Calm down, dear. It can't be that bad.'

'It's only a miserable cookbook,' Evangeline muttered crossly. Martha's voice was ringing out loud and clear. 'It's not *Gone with the Wind.*'

'Please . . .' I waved a shushing hand at Evangeline. 'Now, take a deep breath, dear, and —'

'Ask her about the car,' Evangeline prompted.

'Will you please —'

'Mother, are you there? Are you listening? You're my only hope!'

'I don't like the sound of that,' Evangeline said.

'Oh, shut up!' I didn't like it myself. 'No, not you, darling —'

'Oh, you don't need to tell me that. It's Miss Sinclair, isn't it? Being snide, as usual.'

'I heard that!'

'Go on, darling.' I couldn't deny it. 'I'm listening. What's wrong with Jocasta? She hasn't — ?' That sudden fear for the children had not quite left me. 'She hasn't come down with some awful disease, has she? Something catching?'

'No, no, nothing like that. It's worse. She . . . she hasn't any gas!'

'Most cooks would be pleased about that.' Evangeline just couldn't keep her big mouth shut.

'Please —'

'Not that kind of gas.' Evangeline and Martha were both speaking so loudly that they had no trouble hearing each other. 'The kind you heat your house with. And cook with.'

'Oh-oh . . .' It was becoming clearer now.

'Exactly. We're on a deadline and she's testing all the recipes before we can use them. You know how casual theatre people are about exact amounts and precise directions.'

'Not just theatre people.' I came from a long line of by-guess-and-by-God cooks, who just kept adding ingredients, sometimes substituting, stirring and tasting until they had the results they wanted. Martha was the same, which was obviously why this Jocasta had been brought in as editor.

'Anyway there's a big gas leak some-where in her neighbourhood. The authori-ties have turned off the supplies while they try to trace it, then they'll have to fix it — and heaven knows how long that will take. And we're on a tight deadline. It's all ar-ranged to launch the book at the Lady Lemmings' Autumn Bazaar. So we can't afford to wait until we've collected all the recipes and then test them. We have to test them as we go along — and a good thing, too, Jocasta has already found several that sounded good but were complete disasters when she tried them.'

'And now she can't test anything that needs cooking because there's no gas for her stove.' I had caught up with Martha and, perhaps, was a little ahead of her.

'That's just it, Mother. Ordinarily, we could have just transferred operations to my kitchen, even though it might be a bit awkward with the housekeeper and the children in and out. But Hugh is involved in several new projects and he needs as much peace and quiet on the domestic front as I can provide for him.'

'I quite agree, dear. And you were thinking . . . ?'

'You have that great big modern kitchen there . . .' Martha paused and took a deep breath. 'And you hardly ever use it —'

'I wouldn't say that.' Momentary indignation got the better of me, although I was basically sympathetic to Martha's proposal.

'I mean, you're not there all the time. You eat out a lot. And Jocasta wouldn't be in the way too much. I know all that adulation she has for Miss Sinclair is a bit tedious — but don't worry, once she knows her better she'll get over it.'

Evangeline snorted.

'And it will only be until the gas supply is restored at her place. And you have a full cupboard of spices and all those sauces and gourmet flavourings . . . You wouldn't mind letting her use a bit of them, would you, Mother? For me? She can be over there in half an hour and she'll leave any time it isn't convenient for you.'

'Actually, we're going down to Brighton for a few days, anyway. Tell me, darling, does Jocasta have a car?'

'Of course.'

'Darling!' I exchanged triumphant glances with Evangeline. 'I think we can do a deal.'

Chapter Eight

'Cecile will be a gold mine for you.' Shame-lessly, Evangeline had thrown Dame Cecile to the slavering wolves. Or, in this case, the thrilled, quivering-with-anticipation Jocasta. 'Just bring along your notebook. She's over-flowing with gourmet recipes, theatrical an-ecdotes and all sorts of culinary hints. All on her own, she'll make your book a bestseller. . . . Just give me a hand with these cases, will you, dear?'

The terraces of white wedding cake Re-gency houses curved along streets sloping gently towards the vast grey-blue expanse of the water below. Even though it was a grey day, the glistening white stucco brightened and cheered it.

'Turn here,' Evangeline directed and Jocasta swung the car into a street lined with larger houses, one of which looked fa-miliar.

While I concentrated on getting Cho-Cho's carrier out of the car without jarring her too much, Evangeline soared up the steps to the front door, leaving Jocasta to struggle with the luggage all by herself. No surprise there.

The door opened before we could ring the bell and Soroya stood glaring at us. Especially me.

'About time you brought her back!' She snatched at the carrier, sending Cho-Cho tumbling against the wires with an indignant squawk. 'How dare you go off with my cat like that? I ought to report you to the police!'

'Please, Soroya.' Matilda's weary voice came from behind. 'I told you. I asked Trixie to take the cat out of the way until Cecile had time to calm down.'

'I don't know why you want to have her staying here. I should think you get enough of her at the theatre. It's a rod for your own back.'

Evangeline snorted. When it came to rods, Dame Cecile was the least of them.

'Trixie and Evangeline are going to be staying here for a few days, too.' There was a trace of relish in Matilda's voice as she broke the news.

Soroya opened her mouth, obviously to protest, but noticed the steely glint in Matilda's eyes and shut it again.

'I'll just take the cat up to my room.' She gave me a hostile look. 'Where no one can get at it again.'

'Please do,' Matilda said. 'And keep it out of Cecile's sight. I don't think she's ready to cope with it yet.'

'Still upset, is she?' Evangeline asked heartlessly. After all, Fleur had been with Dame Cecile longer than any of her husbands had.

'Playing it to the hilt.' Matilda shrugged. 'She's taken to going out in the wee hours of the morning and wandering the streets in that black outfit. I wouldn't mind, but she leaves the front door unlocked so that she can get back in. I've had to give her a key — and a good talking-to — but I'm not sure it's worked. The door was on the latch again this morning when I got up.'

Cho-Cho gave a piteous *Meewrrr* and cast me an anguished look as Soroya carried her up the stairs, tilting her cage again and buffeting her against the sides.

'Be careful!' I started forward, hands outstretched to steady the carrier.

'Don't tell *me* how to handle my cat!' Soroya yanked it away, sending Cho-Cho sprawling sideways.

Yeoowrr! This time Cho-Cho's protest was louder and growing angry. She was not accustomed to this treatment — another reason to doubt Soroya's claim that the cat was hers.

'Do be quiet!' Matilda looked nervously towards the top of the stairs. 'You'll disturb Cecile and she'll have another fit if she sees that cat.'

'Your friend Cecile did not return to the house until just before dawn this morning,' Soroya informed her frostily. 'She'll sleep for hours yet. You'll be lucky if she makes the rehearsal this afternoon.' Soroya flounced up the stairs, jouncing Cho-Cho on every step.

A loud thump at the front door startled us all. It sounded as though something had been thrown against it. Matilda crossed the hall swiftly and looked through the small window panel.

'You have some luggage?' she asked.

'Good heavens, Jocasta!' I rushed to open the door. 'I'd forgotten all about her.'

'She must be used to that,' Evangeline murmured.

'I'm so sorry, I stumbled,' Jocasta gasped. 'I hope it hasn't scratched the paint.' We both looked at the oversized suitcase leaning drunkenly against the door. Neither of us quite dared to look at the paint.

'No, no, it's all right,' Matilda reassured her, then frowned uneasily. 'Er . . . are you staying here, too?'

'Oh, no. I just drove them down.' Jocasta resumed her struggle with the cases, heaving them one by one into the hall. 'I'll be going back to London soon. But first, Miss Sinclair promised me that Dame Cecile . . .' She looked around hopefully.

'All in good time.' Evangeline avoided her eyes. 'Now, if you'll just take these cases upstairs, Matilda will show you where to put them.'

'Oh . . . yes . . . of course.' Jocasta looked despairingly at the pile of luggage and the stairs.

'I'll take my own.' I felt guilty about the grateful smile Jocasta gave me, my case was the smallest of the lot.

'This way.' Matilda gamely picked up the next-smallest of the remaining cases, staggering slightly under its weight. I thought I heard a muffled clank from it. I shot Evangeline a sharp look, but she still wasn't meeting anyone's eyes.

'So kind . . .' she said vaguely, drifting towards the drawing room with an abstracted air. 'If you'll excuse me . . . I'll just . . .' She wafted out of sight. '. . . urgent telephone call . . .'

The fact that it was true didn't make me any less annoyed. I tightened my lips and hoped that Superintendent Thursby would not make it easy for her, then followed Matilda up the stairs and down the long hallway, wondering which door Cho-Cho had disappeared behind.

'I thought you might like this room.' Matilda swung open a door. 'It's small, but it has a sea view. Well, actually, it's the English Channel, but it's part of the sea.'

'It's lovely!' It was a jewel box of a room. Small, yes, but light and airy, with a tiny white-painted wrought-iron balcony outside the window, flower-sprigged drapes and bedspread, even a curved recess holding display shelves built into one corner, the curved background painted a delicate shell pink. Fresh flowers stood in cut-glass vases on the dresser and the bedside table. The blue-grey stretch of water cresting the horizon outside was a bonus that would pay dividends on a sunny day.

'Lovely . . .' A wistful echo came from the doorway where Jocasta looked longingly into the room.

'Evangeline's room is opposite, across the hall, you can see it if you come this way.' Matilda threw open a door and apologized. 'You'll have to share a bathroom, I'm afraid. This establishment doesn't run to separate en-suites.'

'Why should it? It isn't a hotel.' I

stepped into a spacious bathroom which had obviously once been another full-sized room connecting the two end-of-corridor rooms and was promptly lost in the nostalgia it evoked. It brought back memories of my first trip to Europe on one of the old liners. Back in the days when 'Jet Set' had been the newly minted description to denote the height of luxury and ocean liners were the old hat, bog standard way of travelling. In those days each third-class cabin had housed four passengers, two up and two down, so eight of us shared the bathroom between every two cabins and, sure as fate, someone always forgot to unlock the door to the opposite cabin when they had finished, so someone else was always hammering on the door, trying to make themselves heard in the cabin on the other side of the bathroom.

'It's all right, so long as you remember to unlatch the other door when you're through,' Matilda said, as though reading my mind. Or perhaps from long experience.

'That won't be a problem,' I said truthfully. Evangeline was highly unlikely to even notice the latch on the opposite door and I wasn't bothered, either. In fact, in view of the delicate negotiation we might be entering into to effect Eddie's release, it would be quite convenient to be able to consult with each other without the rest of the household knowing.

'Good.' Matilda turned away briskly. 'I'll just see to a few other things, then. Cecile really ought to be stirring, if she wants to get to rehearsal on time.'

'I won't disturb you,' Jocasta told me earnestly. 'I'll bring Miss Sinclair's things in through the hall door. Why don't you lie down and have a rest? It was a long drive down.'

She looked as though she were the one in need of a rest; she had done the driving. I smiled agreement and closed my door firmly, then went over to the window to enjoy the view.

It took Jocasta three trips to cart all of Evangeline's luggage up into her room. Cravenly, I kept out of the way, enjoying the panorama of coastal shipping along the Channel. So timeless, so peaceful, so —

'There you are, you wretched creature! Where have you been?' The explosion of Soroya's wrathful tirade banished all thoughts of peace. 'You're late! Days late! Where have you been? If Matilda doesn't report you to your agency, I will! You have no right to treat people like this. You were

engaged in good faith and you have betrayed our trust . . .'

Oh, no! I hurried to the door and threw
it open. As I had feared, poor Jocasta was
quailing against the wall, horrified at being
accosted by what seemed to be a madwoman accusing her of she knew not what.

'No! No! No!' Matilda rushed down the
hallway towards us. 'She has nothing to do
with the agency. She's with Trixie and
Evangeline!'

'That housekeeper still hasn't turned
up?' I deduced, putting an arm around
Jocasta's quivering shoulders.

'I've given up hope. What can you do?'
Matilda shrugged resignedly. 'One makes
all the arrangements. They promise they'll
take the job, they even seem enthusiastic.
Then they never show up. It happens all
the time. But I had such hopes for Mrs
Temple; she was older than the usual run
of applicants and she seemed so responsible. I thought I could depend on her. But
all Australians take these domestic jobs to
finance their Grand Tours and I suppose
she got a chance to join her friends on an
exciting trip and just took off. I wish she'd
let me know, though.'

'Irresponsible!' Soroya sniffed. 'Utterly,
totally irresponsible. Typical. You must

115

phone the agency and demand a replace-
ment — and don't let them charge you another fee, either!'

'Soroya,' Matilda sighed. 'The show is
opening on Monday. I don't have time to
interview staff.'

'You needn't concern yourself with that.
I can easily take such domestic chores out
of your —'

The icy flash in Matilda's eyes stopped
her dead.

'Thank you, but *I* shall decide who pre-
sides over the housekeeping arrangements
in *my* house!'

'That's all very well,' Soroya ignored her
resentment, 'but what are we to do about
meals? I'm getting very tired of going out
to find a restaurant every time I'm hungry.
And you should be, too. It would be far
more restful for you to be able to have your
meals and relax in the privacy of your own
home. Why, there isn't even anything for
lunch today —'

'We can manage,' Matilda said wearily.

'Manage! You've invited a whole
houseful of people to stay indefinitely —
and there isn't even anything in the fridge
for lunch!'

'If it's a question of lunch —' Jocasta
pulled away from my sheltering arm before

I could restrain her — 'perhaps I could help out. I'm rather good at making something from nothing.'

'You don't know what you're getting into,' I warned softly. 'When she says there's nothing in the fridge, she means nothing.'

'There are plenty of supermarkets around and she has a car.' Soroya bestowed a gracious smile on Jocasta. 'So kind of you, my dear.'

Perhaps. And perhaps there was also an ulterior motive. Dame Cecile had not surfaced yet and Jocasta was, quite rightly, afraid that Evangeline would dismiss her and send her back to London before she had a chance to discover that her prospective gold mine contained only fool's gold.

'I *do* appreciate it.' Matilda smiled gently. 'Thank you so much.'

'I'll just take a quick look at what you've got and make out a shopping list to supplement it,' Jocasta said confidently, more comfortable now that she had found a role for herself here.

'I'll show you where everything is.' Matilda led the way to the kitchen and I followed in their wake. I figured Jocasta was going to need all the moral support she could get when she saw the state of that fridge. And I was right.

'Oh, my!' She went pale as she opened the door and paler still as she scanned the contents. I noticed that there was something that seemed to have grown a beard since I had seen it the other day.

'The freezer . . .' Jocasta opened the freezer compartment door and slammed it shut again quickly, but not before I had seen what appeared to be an overgrown snowball lurking in the far corner behind a screen of icicles.

'There must be more than this around!' She looked at me in disbelief.

I shrugged. I wouldn't have bet on it.

'The larder?' Jocasta lived in hope. She was actually asking Matilda.

'I don't think we have one.' Matilda looked around vaguely.

'What about a root cellar?' They both looked at me blankly. So much for trying to be helpful. 'You know,' I elucidated, 'where you keep potatoes, onions, carrots, beets — root vegetables.'

'There's a coal cellar,' Matilda said. 'But we haven't used it since the Clean Air Act came in all those years ago and we switched to gas-fired central heating. I don't know what's down there now.'

'It's worth a try.' Jocasta was not going to give up. She strode forward determinedly.

'There might be the washing machine and dryer.' Matilda did not sound entirely convinced.

'The light switch doesn't seem to work.' Jocasta was fumbling at the wall inside the door. 'Have you a torch?'

'I have a flashlight in my bag.' I began delving for it. Matilda was looking blank again. 'It's tiny, I'm afraid.' I handed it to Jocasta apologetically. 'It's really just for reading theatre programmes and suchlike, but it might be better than nothing.'

'It will do.' Jocasta switched it on and began flashing it about in the darkness behind the door. 'Oh!' She recoiled abruptly. 'The steps are broken! What a good thing I didn't go rushing down there without a light!'

'No one ever goes there,' Matilda said, meaning that she didn't.

'Watch out!' I warned. Jocasta was leaning into the dark opening again.

'I'll be careful.' She advanced cautiously. 'It's just that I think I can see . . .' She disappeared from sight and I gathered myself to follow.

'Do you have any matches?' I wasn't quite silly enough to go after her without any light at all.

'Matches?' Matilda echoed blankly.

'They're dangerous —'

There was a piercing scream from below.

'What is it? Are you all right?' I rushed to the door, then fell back as Jocasta stumbled into view.

'Oh, my!' She moved slowly. 'Oh, my!' There was a pale green tint around her gills. I rescued my flashlight from her trembling hands before she dropped it.

'What is it?' Matilda snapped out of her former abstraction enough to register that something must be wrong.

'Oh, my! . . . Oh, my!' Jocasta faced her and fought visibly to control her shaking body, her sagging knees.

'Easy . . .' I rushed forward to steady her. 'What's the matter?'

'Oh, my!' She clung to me, still staring at Matilda. 'I think I've just found your missing housekeeper.'

Chapter Nine

'I thought the seaside was supposed to be healthy,' Evangeline complained bitterly. 'You can't prove it by us. Every time we come near this benighted town, someone else is dead.'

'City,' Matilda corrected automatically. 'It was created a city for the Millennium Year. It's not a town any more, it's the City of Brighton-and-Hove now.'

'Call it what you like — it's deadly!' Evangeline shot her a nasty look.

Jocasta gave a muffled sob. I was worried about her. She appeared to be going to pieces — and Martha would be furious with me if her recipe-tester and editor were unable to carry on.

'Finish your brandy,' Evangeline instructed her curtly. 'You can have another if that doesn't work.' Evangeline had magicked up a bottle of brandy from seemingly nowhere as soon as she discovered the emergency, proving that I had been right about that clanking suitcase.

'True . . . true . . .' Dame Cecile

moaned. 'There's nothing but death, desolation and despair in this terrible place. I wish I'd never set foot in it!'

'Ready for a top-up, Cecile?' Evangeline didn't wait for a reply and Dame Cecile didn't try to deter her. 'Anyone else?'

We all held out our glasses mutely. It occurred to me that it might not create the best impression if the summoned police walked in to find us rapidly approaching intoxication, but I didn't care. We had a right to be upset.

'This is all very well,' Soroya complained, but not until her glass had been replenished. 'But what about lunch? I'm starving.'

So was I. We looked towards Jocasta hopefully. The show must go on, and all that.

'I'm sorry.' Jocasta had been raised in a tradition of duty and it clearly pained her to forsake it, but she was adamant. 'I can't face food right now. I can't even bear to think about it. I may never cook again!'

Martha was going to kill me. No doubt about it. No matter that it was really Evangeline's fault. I'd have been perfectly happy to have taken the train to Brighton, leaving Jocasta peacefully testing recipes in our kitchen.

'You could still do the shopping,' Soroya suggested. 'The police won't mind if you leave, you're the only one who doesn't have anything to do with the house.'

'She found the body,' Evangeline pointed out.

'I still don't see why you had to call the police.' Soroya had not finished complaining. I was beginning to realize that she never finished. 'A simple accident has nothing to do with them. Matilda's doctor could do anything necessary.'

'Unless the deceased was his own patient and he had seen her recently, any doctor would be obliged to notify the police,' Evangeline informed her. 'We've just eliminated the middle man.'

'You seem to know a lot about it . . . for an actress.' Soroya looked at her suspiciously. May she never find out just how much we both knew about such things.

'After all those murders I solved in *The Happy Couple*, that's not surprising,' Evangeline said.

I breathed a sigh of relief, which was premature. Evangeline might not be going to admit our previous experience, but there was still trouble in the air.

'I've heard of that series,' Soroya said, 'but I'm afraid it was before my time. I was too young —' Trouble was here.

'Not if you were married to Gervaise Jordan!' Evangeline snarled.

'I was very young when I married dear Gervaise,' Soroya sighed. 'Very young — and very much in love. Or else I would have thought twice about saddling myself with an ungrateful stepdaughter. And such a wild, unruly child!'

'I was forty-six at the time,' Matilda snapped. 'She hustled the old fool to a Registry Office before I could intercept them.'

The doorbell's sharp demanding peal suddenly cut through the growing atmosphere. I wasn't the only one who jumped.

'I don't know why you don't get that replaced by some proper chimes,' Soroya complained. 'Perhaps something with a nice tune.'

The bell rang again. Someone was impatient. We all looked at each other. No one made a move.

'It's the housekeeper's job to answer the door!' Jocasta said and began to laugh wildly.

'She's hysterical,' Soroya said. 'Someone slap her face!'

'She's not accustomed to finding dead bodies.' Evangeline was not being sympathetic, just contrary. Ordinarily, the slap-

ping suggestion would have come from her
— and Jocasta would have been lucky if it
had been just a suggestion.

'I'll get the door.' Matilda started forward as it became apparent that no one
else was going to. The bell pealed again.

'Who *is* accustomed to it?' Soroya demanded.

'A little more brandy —' Evangeline
sidestepped the question — 'and she'll be
fine.'

'. . . along here . . .' We heard Matilda's
voice and the tread of heavy feet down the
hallway. 'I'm afraid the only way to reach it
is through the kitchen. If you don't count
the coal hole in the pavement outside . . .'
They moved out of hearing.

'It was so awful!' Jocasta shuddered and
took a deep gulp from her glass. 'The way
she just sprawled there . . . and . . . and
. . .' She took another gulp. 'You didn't see
it all . . .' She turned to me accusingly.
'You didn't take a proper look.'

'I didn't need to. The smell —' I broke
off. Jocasta didn't need reminding.

Evangeline stepped forward quickly and
refilled glasses all round. I tried to catch
her eye as she got to Jocasta, but couldn't.

'May I come in?' We had not noticed the
policeman standing in the doorway. He

wasn't in uniform, but his bearing was unmistakable; he was the man in charge. How long had he been standing there? I tried to remember what we had been saying. Nothing incriminating, I was sure. I relaxed a little.

'And who are you?' In Matilda's temporary absence, Soroya was going to play Lady of the House.

'I . . .' He didn't like being challenged, but he dutifully produced an identification card and handed it to her. 'I am Superintendent Thursby.'

'Thursby!' Evangeline swept forward, brushing Soroya aside, both hands outstretched in welcome. 'Ron Heyhoe's friend! How kind of you to come so quickly. We only spoke a short while ago. Did you bring Eddie with you?'

'I'm afraid I'm here on your other little matter.' He caught her hands smoothly, perhaps as much to restrain her as to greet her. 'And I'm afraid I wasn't able to do anything about your Eddie. When I went to see about it, he'd already been released on bail.'

'Bail?' Evangeline echoed blankly. 'But how? So soon?'

'It appears that he had some high-powered legal beagles at his beck and call. Odd, the arresting officers were of the opinion that he didn't seem the type. Unless he's mixed up in a lot more than we know about.'

'Don't be silly,' Evangeline said. 'He's a taxi driver. *Our* taxi driver. Where is he now?'

'That would be very interesting to know. Along with a few other things —'

'Er . . .' I cleared my throat and smiled ingratiatingly. It looked as though it was time to 'fess up. 'Actually, I rang Hugh before we left London. To see if he could do anything about Eddie. Obviously, he could.'

'You might have told me!' The look Evangeline sent me was glacial. Superintendent Thursby didn't look best pleased, either.

'He may be out on bail,' Thursby said. 'But he isn't allowed to leave town. They tell me he was quite upset about that.'

'You may come in,' Soroya announced majestically, if somewhat belatedly, returning his identification card.

'Thank you, madam.' He advanced farther into the room and took one penetrating look around, not missing the brandy glasses and the level of the liquid in them.

'You ladies were all here when it happened, I take it?' He was all business now, Eddie dismissed, intent on the problem here.

'Not when it *happened*, no,' Evangeline said. *'We —'* she indicated Jocasta and myself — 'drove down from London this morning. We've barely arrived. I understand the housekeeper has been missing for several days. The accident must have happened last week. When we were still in London.'

I wouldn't have pushed it so strongly if I'd been her. If the police discovered we actually had been in Brighton with Eddie recently, they might take a dim view. I wondered just how much liaison there was between local police stations. If we were lucky, we might never find out.

'I stand corrected. What I meant to say was —' He swept a laser-like gaze over us again — 'when the body was discovered.'

Jocasta gave a little moan and dived back into her glass. Everyone except Soroya looked at her sympathetically.

'And this is the lady who found it?' He was quick on the uptake, moving towards Jocasta before we had stopped nodding agreement.

'It was awful,' Jocasta moaned. 'Terrible! I've never seen anything like it in my life.'

I wished I could say that.

'Yes, very shocking for you. Do you feel able to answer a few questions now?'

'But I don't know anything. I was just about to prepare lunch for everyone, but there wasn't anything in the fridge. I . . . I thought I might find some stores in the basement. You know, vegetables, preserves, perhaps tins of meat or fish.' Her voice was growing stronger as she reeled off the comforting litany of familiar foods. 'That sort of thing.'

'Lunch!' Evangeline was reminded. 'We haven't had anything to eat. How long must we stay here? We're starving!'

'And I have to get back to London.' Jocasta was still clinging desperately to a world she knew. 'I have a lot of work to do today before a very important meeting with my collaborator in the morning.'

It took me a moment to realize she was talking about Martha.

'And I have to be at the theatre this afternoon for a run-through,' Dame Cecile announced. 'And so,' she added as an afterthought, 'does Matilda.'

'All in good time, ladies,' he soothed, then turned back to Jocasta. 'Now . . . you were hoping to find some food supplies in the cellar . . .'

Jocasta stared into space.

'You went to the cellar door,' he prompted, 'opened it and . . . ?'

'An' I tried to switch the light on, but it wouldn' work.' She seemed to become aware that she was beginning to slur her words the tiniest bit. She pulled herself up and began to speak with elecutory precision.

'I didn't want to go down the steps in the dark and . . . and there was a strange smell. As if any vegetables stored down there had begun to rot and wouldn't be fit to eat . . . Eat . . .' She retched slightly. 'I may never eat again!'

'That's all very well for you,' Soroya snapped, 'but the rest of us want our lunch. How much longer are you going to keep us here?' she demanded of Thursby. 'Just because some clumsy servant has fallen downstairs and killed herself?'

'All in good time.' Thursby gave her a look that should have stopped an elephant in its tracks, but Soroya was oblivious.

'It has nothing to do with us. We've never even seen the woman! My daughter was fool enough to hire her — and now look at the way it's turned out!' She was in full Memsahib-from-Hell flow and I saw what Matilda meant.

'How was Matilda to know the woman

was unsteady on her feet?' Dame Cecile came to her co-star's defence. 'It's not the sort of thing that shows up in an interview.'

'Nosso cl'msy . . . coulda happ'n any—' Jocasta halted and took a deep breath.

'It could have happened to anyone,' she declaimed clearly. 'Trixie brought me a torch, we could see that the top step was broken. Those stairs were in a dangerous condition.'

'I knew Matilda wasn't keeping my house in proper repair!'

Soroya, proved right, was triumphant.

'Matilda is not —' Dame Cecile began.

'Please, ladies!' Thursby, not surprisingly, had snapped to attention at Jocasta's revelation. A light switch that didn't work and a broken top step could add up to more than an accident.

'Matilda —' Dame Cecile began again.

'Right. We can't talk here.' Thursby turned back to Jocasta and offered her a hand to help her rise. 'I'd like to have a word with you in private,' he told her.

'Cer'nly . . .' She rose with great dignity, took two steps forward and crumpled into a heap at his feet.

'Well!' Evangeline could not hide her satisfaction at a job well done. 'So much for her driving back to London this afternoon!'

Chapter Ten

'Mother, I can't believe you let this happen!'
Martha was not taking the news well. I was
relieved that I did not have to face her. The
telephone was so much more comfortable.

'I should have watched Evangeline more
carefully,' I admitted. 'But how was I to
know Jocasta was so unaccustomed to
drink? It isn't very usual these days.'

'Unaccustomed?' Martha gave a sharp
laugh. 'She's practically a teetotaller. She
raises an eyebrow when a recipe calls for a
tablespoon of Cointreau. I'm amazed you
got her to drink anything at all.'

'She was pretty shaken. And Evangeline
just kept pouring. And, darling . . .' I might
as well get the worst over with. 'I don't
think you should count on seeing her at all
tomorrow. Not with the hangover she's
going to wake up with.' In fact, it might be
a couple of days before Jocasta felt anything close to normal, but one unpleasant
fact at a time would be enough for Martha.

'Oh, Mother!'

'Look on the bright side, darling. At

least we've got Eddie out of jail. That bail bondsman Hugh recommended took care of everything in no time.'

'Yes.' Martha's voice softened. 'Hugh is a marvel. Of course, he's had so much experience with unstable actors that he's built up a roster of specialists to handle any emergency.'

'He's just wonderful, darling,' I assured her. 'And Evangeline and I are very grateful to him. Eddie will be, too, when he stops sulking. Poor lamb, it's been one shock after another for him. Especially when he came to find us and saw that the police were here. He went away until they'd gone, then he was in a mood when we wanted some help. He said he was spending his life driving us to supermarkets. But we *had* to go shopping. Talk about a cupboard being bare!'

'Poor Eddie.'

'He's furious because he wants to get to London, but he'll be all right. The house is full, but Matilda has booked him into a small bed-and-breakfast nearby. And Evangeline is going to foot the bill — whether she knows it or not!'

'Good! But, Mother, what can we do about Jocasta? We're on such a tight deadline, we don't have any time to spare. She was supposed to have tested six recipes by now — and she hasn't done one. I should have known better than to let her drive you and Miss Sinclair!' Would that bitterness never leave my poor darling's voice? Poor sweet, how she hated her heritage.

'Darling —'

'Oh, don't worry. I know who to blame. I'm not blaming you.'

'No, darling, and you can't blame Evangeline for something that happened before we arrived on the scene. It was an accident, that's all. Bad luck for everyone concerned.' Especially Mrs Temple, but I thought it better not to say that.

'That's just it! If you weren't there, you wouldn't be concerned. And you've dragged Jocasta into it. And our working schedule calls for us to have Chapter One — "Breakfast Cheer" — finished in twenty-four hours. And we need at least one more recipe — preferably for eggs.'

'Oh, no!' I recoiled in empathy. 'Jocasta isn't going to be able to face an egg for a couple of days.'

'That's what I was afraid of! What do we tell the publisher: Sorry, that editor you assigned to me is too hungover to do her job?'

'That might not surprise them. . . . No,

darling, I didn't mean that. Look, for one recipe, why don't you give them my No-Pans-to-Wash-Poached-Egg?'

'Oh, I haven't thought of that in years! But do you think you can really call it a Breakfast Cheer recipe?'

'I don't see why not. It sure cheers me not to have to scrub sticky egg white off a pan or egg poacher.'

'Yes, you're right. It's just the thing for someone on their own in digs and in a hurry. If I can remember it . . .'

'It's too simple to forget. You just tear off a good-sized piece of clingfilm, drape it over a cup and poke it down to make a well. Oil it lightly, break the egg into it, tie up the ends and lower it into your pan of boiling water. You can even watch it cooking. Just pull it out when it's poached the way you like it, snip off the knot with your kitchen scissors, roll the egg on to your slice of toast, fishcake, corned beef hash, or what have you and throw the clingfilm away. Voilà! No fuss, no mess, no bother — and no washing up!'

'And it's a perfect shape, too.' Martha was right there with me down Memory Lane. 'None of those sprawling tentacles of dripping white you get when you try to poach it in a saucepan. Yes, we can use that.'

'Oh —' I remembered something else. 'It's also a good idea to put a knife over the cup and tie the knot over the knife. Then you can lower the egg into the pan, leaving the knife across the pan and you can lift it out more easily.'

'Wonderful! Every little bit helps. We can give it a page to itself, perhaps with little sketches around it. You know, Mother, I'm not sure I should have started this. I expected Jocasta to be more help than she has been so far.'

'Give her time, darling. Even if she can't go back to London in the morning, perhaps she can do a bit of experimenting in the kitchen here. With everyone constantly in and out, this household is going to need odd meals at odd times. There'll be plenty of scope for one-dish cooking.'

If, that is, Jocasta felt able to face food again so soon. I tried to ignore the spectre of reality tugging at my sleeve. More to the point, if she were able to face preparing it in that kitchen with the door to the cellar a constant reminder. No, perhaps better not mention such thoughts to Martha. She was happy now.

'Tell Jocasta to ring me as soon as she surfaces,' Martha directed. 'At least we can have a telephone consultation before she gets back to town. And, Mother — look after yourself. I don't like the way things are going in Brighton.'

'Accidents will happen, that's all, darling, and we just have to live with it. You look after yourself, too, and give my love to Hugh and the children.'

'Yes, well . . .' Obviously, she wanted to add more, but I heard a voice calling her in the distance. 'Yes, yes, I'm coming. Goodnight, Mother.'

I hung up the phone with a feeling of relief. It could have been worse. It might be yet. But, in the famous line from one of the roles I didn't get, 'I'll worry about it tomorrow.'

As I turned out the light, I became uneasily aware of just how dark and silent the rest of the house was. Unusually so, for a place full of theatre people. Of course, Matilda and Dame Cecile had had a tiring rehearsal to cap a busy and emotionally exhausting morning; it was not surprising that they had retired to their rooms early. Evangeline had last been seen heading towards her own room, clutching her cellphone and murmuring about a consultation with her financial adviser. If that meant Nigel, I didn't want to know about it. As for Soroya — who cared?

Actually the house wasn't all that silent. It muttered to itself with the creaks and groans of an old building settling down for the night. All right if you were used to it, as Matilda was, but subtly unnerving, if you weren't. I told myself that Matilda would have had the courtesy to warn us if the place was haunted, but it was that time of darkness when anything seemed possible. And perhaps the ghost was so recent that no one was aware of it yet.

What about that new housekeeper, starting a new job, looking forward to an interesting new life, suddenly finding herself plunging down a dark staircase into oblivion? Would her disgruntled shade still be hanging around to . . . exact some sort of revenge?

That was the front door! I sat bolt upright. The muffled slam sounded as though a sudden gust of wind had snatched the door from someone's furtive grasp.

Someone going out . . . or someone coming in?

I seemed to hold my breath for an endless time, straining to hear more, wondering if there were more to hear. Was that creak someone coming up the stairs, or just another complaint from the old house?

Silence . . . silence . . . I had to breathe. I

took a great choking gasp. Then it was just a gasp as my doorknob rattled. Why hadn't I locked the door? Why had I been such a trusting fool? Had experience taught me nothing? A woman had died in this house — and recently. The broken top step was no guarantee that it had been an accident.

I saw the door move slowly, but there was no dark shadow visible against the outer darkness. I braced myself. Fight or flight? Or should I let out a few loud healthy screams? What if it was someone innocent and I roused the household?

'Evangeline . . . ?' I whispered hopefully.

Silence . . . The door began to swing shut again. Was someone inside the room? Or had I frightened them away?

'Evangeline . . . ?' I whispered again, without hope. The bed shook abruptly — and it wasn't me.

'*Prrrryaaah!*' The soft triumphant cry acted like a knife blade slicing through the strings that had held me taut. I fell back on the pillows limply.

'*Prrr . . . prrrr . . .*' A throbbing furry bundle of delight rubbed against me, nuzzling my neck, my chin, my cheeks.

'You clever little darling, you found me!' I hugged Cho-Cho to me. 'Oh, you *are* a clever girl!'

'*Prrryaaah* . . .' She trilled agreement.

'But . . . how did you get away from Soroya?'

She wasn't telling. She snuggled close, purring her little head off, and settled down for the night.

That was fine with me. I curled my arms around her and, with that soft comforting purr drowning out any more creaks or groans, fell into a dreamless sleep.

Chapter Eleven

'I'm dying,' Jocasta whimpered. 'Go away and let me die in peace.'

'Nonsense!' Evangeline wasn't usually up this early herself but, in this case, she had made an exception. 'They say the best thing is a full cooked breakfast —'

'Aaaargh! I can never eat again!'

'Then the next best thing is the hair of the dog that bit you.'

'I will never drink again!'

'If you don't eat and you don't drink,' Evangeline pointed out, 'you *will* die.'

'Exactly. Go away and let me get on with it.'

'Evangeline, come away and leave her alone,' I said. 'She'll feel better after a few hours' more sleep.'

'Sleep! I can't sleep! I've got to get back to London! What time is it?' Jocasta tried to sit up, but slumped back clutching her head and moaning. 'I can't move.'

'Have you noticed how little stamina young people have these days?' Evangeline asked me. 'They can't do anything.'

Jocasta raised her head feebly and glared at Evangeline. I got the feeling that she had just resigned from the Evangeline Sinclair Fan Club.

'And —' She transferred the glare to me and Cho-Cho, who was advancing daintily, nose twitching, to explore this new territory. 'And make that cat stop stamping its feet!'

'Come on.' I stooped and swept Cho-Cho into my arms. 'Let's go downstairs. Evangeline, come along.' I moved aside to let her out of the room first. I didn't trust her not to slam the door. I closed it quietly.

'I suspect this is Jocasta's first hangover,' I said, as we entered the kitchen. 'And it's a lulu!'

'Don't worry, I can take care of that.' Evangeline went to the cupboard and removed a couple of small items before crossing to the fridge and taking out one of the bottles of champagne we'd bought yesterday.

With a plaintive mew, Cho-Cho twisted free of my arms and plunged across the room to paw at the fridge.

'Do you suppose that wretched woman hasn't fed her?' Evangeline looked down at the frantic cat, now wrapping itself around her ankles.

'She probably didn't. Poor Cho-Cho must be starving.' I started for the cupboard where I had stored the half-dozen little tins of gourmet cat food that I had picked up at the supermarket, but Evangeline was faster.

She opened the fridge again, took out the salmon and broccoli quiche I had earmarked for lunch, tore off a large chunk and, without bothering about such niceties as a bowl or saucer, tossed it to the floor.

Cho-Cho pounced on it, also untroubled by the informality. She really was starved, she was even eating the broccoli.

Evangeline returned to business. I watched with fascination as she took a cube of sugar and saturated it just short of disintegration point with Angostura bitters.

'What are you doing?' I gasped, as she poured a heap of cayenne pepper into a saucer and rolled the sugar cube in it, coating it liberally with cayenne. She then dropped it into a champagne flute, popped open the bottle and filled the flute with champagne.

'One from the old days. Best hangover cure-cum-pick-me-up I know,' she said cheerfully, watching as the bubbles began to rise from the sugar cube.

'Pick-me-up? It looks more like a scrapeme-off-the-ceiling to me!' Each bubble was carrying grains of cayenne towards the surface, turning the golden liquid a light reddish brown.

'Now get that up to Jocasta and stand over her until she drinks every drop. That will put her back on her feet.'

'Or under the table permanently,' I muttered. Trust Evangeline to know the recipe for a hangover cure, if nothing else. Still, Martha might be able to use it and, since Jocasta had the hangover, she could test the recipe — which was what she was supposed to do, anyway.

Fortunately, Jocasta was in too weak a condition to put up any fight when I eased her upright and put the glass into her hand. She was at the thirsty stage and had gulped half the liquid before the cayenne kicked in and jolted her eyes wide open.

'What *is* this?' she choked.

'A little concoction of Evangeline's,' I said. 'Drink up. She swears it will do you a world of good.'

'I'm not so sure.' Jocasta sipped gingerly. 'What's in it?'

'Evangeline will give you the recipe for the book later. Right now, just consider that you're testing it.'

Jocasta took another sip and smiled

wanly. 'And I thought I wouldn't be able to do any work today.'

Evangeline was studying the nearly full champagne bottle thoughtfully when I got back to the kitchen.

'I told you we ought to get some half bottles. Now you've got all that left over.'

'It won't be wasted.' Evangeline gestured to the carton of orange juice on the table. 'Buck's Fizzes all round, I think. Just right for a good start to the day.'

There were more champagne flutes on the table. She quarter-filled two of them with orange juice, topped them up to just below the rim with champagne and handed one to me.

'Oh, well, why not?' I set Jocasta's empty glass, with its little sludge of undissolved sugar and cayenne at the bottom, down on the table and accepted my own drink. Cho-Cho was drinking milk — from a saucer, I was relieved to note.

'Ah, another customer.' Evangeline greeted Dame Cecile as she appeared in the doorway 'Buck's Fizz for lunch, Cecile?' She began pouring.

'You know how to live, Evangeline.' Dame Cecile's eyes lit up. 'I always did say that about you.'

'Along with several other things, no doubt.'

'Only when you were particularly insufferable.'

They exchanged small wry smiles. It looked as though a truce was being declared.

I removed the quiche from the fridge, along with the makings of a salad. 'Do you like your quiche hot or cold, Cecile?' I asked.

It was a reasonable question, but she did not appear to think so. An arctic blast froze me as she swept her icy gaze over me and then Cho-Cho. The truce did not extend to us.

After brunch, Evangeline went off to the theatre with Dame Cecile and Matilda. I stayed behind, still feeling vaguely responsible for Jocasta. Someone should be around when she surfaced again. I intended to make sure she ate something before she faced the long drive back to London. I also intended to try to persuade her to stay another night before she got behind the wheel of a car again.

Also, to tell the truth, I didn't want to leave Cho-Cho-San. We had little enough time left together before Evangeline and I went back to London, leaving her to whatever tender mercies Soroya might possess.

Come to think of it, we hadn't seen Soroya all morning. I'd gathered it was unusual for her to miss a meal, but there had been no sign that she had had an early breakfast — and no one was complaining because she hadn't joined us for brunch.

I wondered whether it had been Soroya I had heard closing the front door in the early hours of the morning. If she had left her room silently, not noticing Cho-Cho slipping out at her feet, it would explain how Cho-Cho had escaped to find me.

I wasn't going to worry about Soroya. Jocasta would feel better when she awoke and, for the moment, Cho-Cho was safe and happy with me.

If I put my mind to it, I could probably find quite a few other matters to worry about, but I wasn't in the mood. Outside, the sky was blue and beckoning, light breezes stirred the budding trees, the sun was warm. Spring was in the air and the old-fashioned teak deck chairs stretched out invitingly in a corner of the deck, just beyond the wrought-iron table and upright chairs. I eyed them thoughtfully.

'If I take you outside,' I said to Cho-Cho, 'you won't run away, will you? You'll stay with me?'

She seemed to understand. She hurled herself again at my ankles, purring enthusiastically, then danced over to the door and waited for me to open it.

We settled ourselves in a deck chair in the sun and closed our eyes. The fresh sea air reminded me of how much I had missed while living in town. Impressive and historic though the Thames might be, it didn't have the same tang to it.

I think I was almost asleep when Cho-Cho stirred suddenly in my lap and sat up. Then I heard the soft tread of feet on the steps leading up to the deck. I sat bolt upright and twisted around.

'Eddie!' I hadn't realized how uptight I was until I went limp with relief. 'I thought you were driving Evangeline and Dame Cecile to the theatre.'

'Naw . . . 'aven't seen 'em. 'Aven't 'eard a peep from anybody all day. Walked along the seafront. Walked out to the end of the pier and back.' He was bored and aggrieved. 'Then decided I might as well make myself useful.' He swung a small toolkit he was carrying. 'So I picked up a few things at the DIY centre and thought I'd come over 'ere and fix those cellar stairs for you lot. Can't leave 'em the way they are, they're dangerous.'

'Are you allowed to?' I wondered. 'I mean, don't the police want them left the way they are?'

'Why should they? They say anything about that to you? They sealed the area off with those tapes?'

'Well, no . . .' I admitted. 'I just thought . . .'

'Not in accident cases.' He frowned at me, then forgave me. 'Trouble with you is, you've got mixed up in too much nasty business lately. You can't believe in ordinary accidents any more. You let your imagination run away with you and go looking for trouble.'

'That fire at the taxidermist's wasn't my imagination,' I said. 'Was the dead body your imagination?'

'That was there, this is 'ere.' Eddie didn't want to talk about that. The police questioning had exhausted everything he had to say on that subject. He started for the kitchen door.

'Sit down a minute,' I said. 'Jocasta is still asleep and she's in no condition to have anyone doing any hammering around the house.'

'Like that, is it?' Eddie sank into the other deck chair, nodding sagely. 'She'll have to toughen up if she's going to hang

149

around with you lot.'

'She's hanging around with Martha, actually. They're working on a cookbook together. We only have her with us now because . . . well, because she's got a car and we needed to get down here quickly because you . . .'

'Right. An' I'm in this whole mess because of you two.' He stared glumly into the distance, then his eyes abruptly focused and sharpened. 'Oi! What's 'e doing 'ere?'

I turned and saw Nigel coming up the steps.

'Ah! I thought I heard voices,' he greeted us.

'Don't open your purse,' Eddie muttered to me.

'Don't worry,' I muttered back before I raised my voice to return the greeting. 'This is a surprise, Nigel. Having a day at the seaside?'

'Ah! Yes. I had business to transact nearby and I thought, while I was here, I'd drop in on you and . . .' He looked around hopefully. 'Evangeline?'

'Not here at the moment, I'm afraid. She and Dame Cecile went off to the theatre and I don't know where else.'

'Ah! She'll be back soon?' He was losing

hope, but still in there trying.

'She didn't say — and I wouldn't even guess at a time. You know what they're like when they get together.'

'Ah!' He squinted up at a passing cloud and spoke with elaborate casualness. 'She, ah, didn't happen to leave anything for me to pick up, did she?'

'Not that I know of.' So Nigel hadn't happened to drop in on the spur of the moment. I remembered Evangeline's telephone calls yesterday. Something had been arranged between them — or he thought it had. Evangeline had obviously not been so sure — or had changed her mind.

'Ah!' He frowned and sank down on one of the wrought-iron chairs. 'Perhaps I might wait a while? She might come back . . .'

'She might.' More likely she might not. 'Make yourself at home.'

' 'E already 'as,' Eddie muttered.

'How's your uncle?' I decided to change to a safer subject. Or was it?

'Uncle? Uncle?' Nigel might never have heard the word before. He looked around wildly.

'Uncle,' I repeated firmly. 'You know, the one with the legendary lost theatre underneath the arches.'

'Ah! Yes. That one.' He looked dismayed,

then brightened. 'Not well. Not too well at all. Rather poorly.' The thought seemed to cheer him. 'Quite poorly, in fact.'

I had the sudden suspicion that he might soon be going to announce that his uncle had died and that the theatre had passed into the hands of a developer and was lost for ever. With even deeper suspicion, I wondered whether he had an uncle at all, or whether he had invented the whole story just to lure us into his financial schemes.

'How *is* business?' I asked.

'Business? Business?' It might be another word he had never heard before, one I had made up just to confuse him.

'You said you were here on business,' I reminded him. 'I hope it went well.'

'Ah! Yes. Well . . . not quite. Nothing that can't be mended with a fresh injection of —' He broke off and looked at me expectantly.

Capital. That sentence finished itself. I'd heard it often enough in my lifetime. Usually just before the big, exciting, sure-thing project went down the Swanee.

'Ah . . . has Evangeline mentioned this investment opportunity to you?' Sure enough, he was in there pitching. 'I believe there might still be just enough time to get you in on the ground floor.'

'Don't do it!' Eddie was Cassandra leading a Greek chorus in the background. 'Whatever it is, don't do it!'

'Don't worry,' I told him. 'With the stock market heading south the way it is, I have no intention of going anywhere near it.' I was surprised that Evangeline had.

'Right. You want to stay away from all them dotty coms.'

'No, no. Nothing to do with the stock market.' Nigel gave a fastidious shudder, curling his fingers in the body language of someone who had been badly burned. 'I've taken my clients out of that. Bricks, not clicks — that's the thing now. If anything should happen, there are still solid assets to cash in — you can't lose. At least,' he added, in a sudden burst of candour, 'not everything.'

'Pack it in, mate!' Eddie advised. 'Next time Trixie's got any spare cash, she's going to set me up in my own 'ire car business.'

'Unfortunately, there's nothing to spare at the moment.' I made it clear. 'Nor likely to be for quite some time. If ever.'

'Ah!' Nigel slumped back in his chair and returned to brooding.

'Well.' Eddie stood and gave me a con-spiratorial wink. 'I'll go and 'ave a look at them stairs for you. Sounds like someone's stirring in there, so it ought to be all right.'

'I'd better see how she is.' There were faint clattering sounds, interspersed with agonized groans coming from the kitchen. 'I still think you ought to keep it quiet. She won't be up to much.' I glanced at the disconsolate Nigel and my heart betrayed me. He didn't look up to much, either.

'Why don't you move into the kitchen?' I suggested. 'I'll fix you a snack while you wait for Evangeline.'

'Ah!' He brightened. 'Too kind of you.'

'Too right, too kind,' Eddie grumbled. 'We were almost rid of 'im.'

'Shush!' Luckily, Nigel did not appear to have heard. Cho-Cho was already at the door, waiting for us.

'Don't let the door slam!' Jocasta pleaded as we trooped into the kitchen. She was slumped at the table, a large glass of water in her trembling hand.

'Like that, is it?' Eddie, who had pursed his lips to begin whistling, unpursed them again and regarded her sympathetically. 'Tried the 'air of the dog yet, 'ave you?'

'Don't even mention it!' Jocasta gave him a hate-filled look and shuddered.

'Sorry I spoke. Only tryin' to be 'elpful.' Eddie marched across the room with a pur-

He seemed a perfectly ordinary, perhaps not too successful, jobbing actor. Probably specializing in character parts and secondary leads. Could someone have hated him enough to want to take revenge by destroying what he held dear?

From the expression on her face at the moment, Dame Cecile was first in the queue of suspects. Except that she had been too caught up in the drama of the expiring Fleur-de-Lys to have been able to plot and carry out such an elaborate revenge. Nor would she have harmed an innocent animal no matter how much its owner had offended her.

Telling myself I wasn't jealous because Cho-Cho appeared to have forgotten my existence, I turned back to the fridge to continue what I had started: putting together some sort of scratch meal for Nigel. Then I stopped and looked again.

Nigel had disappeared. So had Evangeline.

Well, it was her funeral. With a mental shrug, I abandoned the idea of a man-sized meal and turned back to Jocasta, who was flagging visibly.

'How about some tea and toast?'

'Excellent idea,' Dame Cecile said. 'Make it cinnamon toast.'

161

'Dry.' Jocasta shuddered. 'Just some dry toast, please.'

I nodded and paid no attention. When I set the hot buttered toast, liberally sprinkled with sugar and cinnamon in front of her, she ate it without a murmur. Dame Cecile nodded approval and polished off her own portion with relish.

Eddie had drifted off towards the cellar door and squatted down, peering intently into the darkness below.

The only sound in the room was Cho-Cho's purr. It was so quiet, it was almost peaceful. Then, suddenly, everything went wrong, before I could do a thing to stop it.

'We'll be on our way now,' the man said. 'Before you-know-who shows up. Thanks, Cecile. Come on, little darling.' He gave Cho-Cho another nuzzle. 'We're going home.'

Gone. They were gone. I stood frozen as the front door slammed. Behind me, I heard a hiss of sharply indrawn breath from Eddie. Instinctively, I turned towards him, sure of meeting a sympathetic gaze.

But Eddie was now crouched inside the cellar opening, only the top of his head to be seen. Apparently he was three or four steps down and staring intently at the ruined top step.

'Don't like the look of that,' he muttered.

'What?' I crossed over to him.

'Look at this.' He pointed to something I could not see.

'I can't see it from here.' I started forward. 'I'll have to come down and look at it from your level.'

'No!' He held up a hand to stop me. 'Don't come down. It's too dangerous. Look . . .' He indicated a smear along the threshold. 'You can see that, can't you?'

'Yes . . .' Reluctantly, I bent to inspect it. To my relief, it wasn't blood. 'But . . . what is it?'

'Grease.' He ran a finger over it, then sniffed at his fingertip. 'Maybe butter.'

'But there was hardly any butter in the fridge — Oh!'

'All used up on this, I reckon.' He nodded glumly. 'And what you can see from where I'm standing is a lot of nail 'oles — with no nails in them, like the nails were pulled out to make the stair treads unstable. And there's no railing. If the grease didn't get 'er, the broken steps would. Once she started to fall, she didn't 'ave a chance. Don't know what the police were thinking to let it go, the way they did. *I* wouldn't call it an accident.'

'You can't be sure of that!'

'You want to bet I'm wrong?' He met my eyes challengingly. 'Where are all the missing nails, then? An' I reckon someone took a hammer and gave the top step a good bashing to break it up. Loose and broken and greased.' He shook his head. 'They don't make coppers the way they used to.'

'I don't think the police examined it too closely. The broken top step was so obvious, the grease wasn't. And there was no light —'

'No bulb in the socket,' he said. 'Now, if it had been a burnt-out bulb, fair enough. But missing . . . ?'

'What are we going to do?'

'I don't know what you're going to do, but I'm going to fix these stairs before anybody else gets 'urt.'

'But —'

'Don't say it!' he warned. 'I've 'ad enough of the police. 'Aven't you?'

'But —' I didn't want to get involved any more than he did, but it still didn't seem right.

'Trixie!' How long had Evangeline been standing there? 'Tea break is over. We're going back to the theatre now. Are you coming?'

I looked around the kitchen. Dame Cecile

had firmly urged Jocasta out on the deck and into a deck chair where she could nap and get the benefit of the sea air. Eddie had bent again to his self-appointed task and was totally absorbed. The empty saucer on the floor by the fridge made my heart twist.

'Are you?'

'I guess so.' There was nothing left for me here.

Not that there was anything much for me at the theatre, either.

'Places, everyone!' a ringing female voice called out. I had no place. Neither had Evangeline, but it wasn't bothering her. She and Cecile were whispering together in the wings and giggling like schoolgirls . . . naughty schoolgirls. If I'd had enough energy, I'd have feared the worst.

Except that I had the feeling that the worst had already happened to me.

'Places, everyone!' the voice repeated, with a trace of asperity.

Matilda materialized from nowhere to preside at the waiting tea table. A nondescript elderly man appeared and seated himself in an armchair beside her. 'Teddy Roosevelt', easily recognizable as Cho-Cho's friend, despite the large moustache and pince-nez he now wore, moved forward to stand by Matilda's other side.

Instinctively, I looked around for Cho-Cho but, of course, he had said he was taking her home — wherever that might be — not to the theatre. I hoped she was safe there. I didn't like the thought of her being left alone someplace. How many people knew where he lived?

'Teddy! That was your cue!' the voice said sharply. Onstage, the action had begun — or tried to.

'Oh, sorry.' Abstractedly, the actor looked out over the footlights. 'Afraid I was thinking of something else.'

'That was obvious!' The voice betrayed a fraying patience. 'Perhaps you could bring yourself to join the rest of us . . . ?'

'Yes . . . yes . . . Sorry, Frella.'

'From the top!'

I sat back and let the familiar proceedings wash over me. It was a good play and it would have been fun to be up there with Evangeline, playing the leading roles, but I knew I was right. We needed a brand new play we could make our own. We wanted to look forward, not back.

Which brought my thoughts back to Nigel. He had disappeared pretty smartly after his brief conference with Evangeline. It had lasted just about long enough for her to write a cheque. I hoped she knew what she was doing. Rather, what he was doing.

'Teddy! Can't you pay attention?' I winced as the shrill voice soared into the stratosphere. Teddy was fluffing his lines again. I got the impression it wasn't going to augur well for his home life.

'It's always a mistake for an actor to marry his director — even if it's the only way he can get the part.' Slipping into the seat beside me, Evangeline was of the same opinion. 'I hope he has a good understudy — because if she doesn't sack him, one of the other actors is going to murder him.'

'All right . . .' This time the voice was dangerously self-controlled. Teddy had fluffed again. 'Just carry on. Let's get to the end of this scene.'

Something brushed against my ankles, startling me. I gasped and looked down.

A large orange cat looked up at me, blinking huge green eyes.

'Don't be frightened,' a voice said from the row behind. 'It's only Garrick. He may look fierce but, unless you've got four legs, a long tail and a squeak, he's a pussycat.'

'I'm sure of it.' I leaned forward and wriggled my fingers for Garrick to investigate. 'He just startled me, that's all. I didn't expect a cat here.'

'All theatres have a cat. The way actors leave their snacks lying around and audiences drop sweets, the place would be overrun otherwise. We couldn't do without Garrick, he's the best mouser in the business.'

Hearing a familiar voice, Garrick abandoned me and strolled under my seat to the next row.

'Here he is. You know who feeds you, don't you, Garrick?'

I watched Garrick defect without regret. He was a perfectly nice cat, but he wasn't Cho-Cho-San. Equally, I suppose he thought I was a nice enough woman, but I didn't control the tin opener.

'Hello, Jem.' Evangeline also recognized a familiar voice. 'Cecile told me you were stage door keeper here. It's been a long time.'

'The Royal Empire was built in 1809. Sometimes it feels as though I've been here from the beginning.'

'Jem played the odious child brother with Cecile and me in *Three on a Match* way back when,' Evangeline informed me. 'He was brilliant. Everyone had him marked out for a great future.'

'That's the way it goes.' He shrugged.

'Some of us go up, some of us go down. You've done very well for yourself, Evangeline. You and Cecile.'

'But you. You were one of the most promising juveniles in the West End. You should have gone on to romantic leads and matinée idoldom. What happened, Jem?'

'The war, what else?' He shrugged again. 'I was too young to be called up for service, so I went into fire watching. Got caught inside when a building collapsed, but I was lucky, really. Buried in the rubble for more hours than I want to remember, but they dug me out. Thing was, when they carried me to the surface, there were a lot of people watching. An audience. They even burst into applause.

'Strange thing . . . when I recovered, tried to get back to work again, I found I couldn't face an audience. Hated applause. It terrified me.' Another shrug. 'Not the best sort of condition for an actor to be in. Oh, yes, and there was a touch of the old claustrophobia, too. It might have been all right out on the actual stage — if it hadn't been for the audience in the auditorium — but you know how cramped most of the dressing rooms are.'

'Oh, Jem,' Evangeline said softly.

'Yes, well . . . I tried my hand at writing

a few plays, but times had changed. Television was taking over the sort of light polite plays the theatre used to thrive on: the drawing-room comedies, the whodunnits, the eternal triangles. The stage opted for the kitchen sink, the absurd, the surreal, the — if you ask me — bloody incompetent! Oh, I got a few things put on, but they didn't run long, not the way they would have before. They were rather popular with amateur theatre groups, though. In fact, I still get a small but steady income from —'

'How am I supposed to remember my lines if people keep talking all the time?'

'Jem, do you mind?' The icy disembodied voice agreed. Teddy might be petulant, but he had right on his side this time.

'Sorry, got carried away meeting old friends.' Jem stood and moved away. 'Time for me to be getting on with a few duties,' he told us in parting.

'Jem, please —'

I looked around for the source of the voice that kept issuing instructions. The rows of seats behind us were empty now that Jem had left. Even Garrick wasn't to be seen.

'Dress Circle.' Evangeline had spotted her. 'Checking for sound — and she needs to.'

'Shhhhh!' This time it was Dame Cecile shushing us from the wings. It really was time to keep quiet.

We sat in silence as the first act proceeded towards one of the big laughs.

'Charge!' Teddy said languidly and strolled up the staircase.

'Cecile is right,' Evangeline whispered. 'The next words are going to be "to my account".'

'Teddy dear,' the disembodied voice seemed to agree, 'could we have a little more fire? From the foot of the stairs again, please.'

'Faugh!' Teddy got more fire into his exclamation of disgust as he stamped back to the foot of the stairs. The other actors waited more or less patiently. They were obviously accustomed to this.

'Charge!' Unfortunately, the fire didn't last through to his actual line. He did move a little faster up the staircase, though.

'Better,' the voice said wearily. 'But try it again.'

'How long have they been in rehearsal?' I asked *sotto voce,* but it wasn't *sotto* enough.

'Could we please have quiet in the stalls?'

'How can I concentrate with all that babble going on?' It was clear that Teddy was going to blame all his problems on us.

Now everyone was glaring at us.

'Do you get the feeling we're not wanted around here?' Evangeline rose majestically.

'Definitely.' I scrambled to my feet before she pushed past me and stepped all over them.

'*Meeoyaaah!*' How was I to know that Garrick had settled down in the aisle with his tail stretched out across the end of the row? I began to appreciate even more the beauty of a bobtail cat as Garrick streaked for the shelter of the wings, yowling imprecations all the way.

'For God's sake!' Teddy exploded. He had plenty of fire now, but it was all directed at us.

'We are leaving,' Evangeline announced.

'Thank God!' somebody muttered. I couldn't tell who.

Chapter Thirteen

'I think we need a breath of fresh air,' Evangeline decided as we left the theatre.

'And a long walk to calm down,' I agreed.

'I am perfectly calm.' Evangeline gave me a haughty look. 'Which is more than can be said for some. That director is on the verge of a nervous breakdown, as well she might be.'

'It's too bad,' I said. 'Teddy is unbalancing the whole play. No timing, no voice projection, no . . . fire. He should be replaced.'

'Not so easy to do when it's her husband.' Evangeline paused reflectively. 'I hope, for her sake, he has some of that fire she wants in private life. He certainly isn't wasting it on his stage performance.'

'We haven't actually seen her yet,' I said, 'but she sounds a lot more dynamic than he does. Of course, that wouldn't be hard. They seem an oddly matched couple.'

'So many of them are, but she has only herself to blame. He was engaged to another woman when Frella snatched him away. Another strong dominating woman — he seems to go for that type.'

'Or they go for him.' I could see Teddy as the natural prey of dominating women. The guy who couldn't say no. 'I suppose Cecile filled you in on all the gossip.'

'And then some!' Evangeline stopped and quirked an eyebrow at me. 'Would you care to guess who that other woman was?'

'No!' I gasped. There was only one other woman in this scenario who could truly be called domineering. 'Not — ?'

'Soroya!' Evangeline confirmed. 'Not only that — guess what she gave him for an engagement present when *they* became engaged?'

I could only stare at her. My mind was boggling.

'A rare foreign breed of cat — the only known one in this country — she brought back from a location trip to Japan.'

'Cho-Cho-San! So that's why she says the cat belongs to her!'

'She has a point. It used to be customary to return the gifts when the engagement was broken.'

'Hah! I'll bet she didn't return the ring!'

'That's different.' Evangeline was always on the acquisitive side. '*He* was the one who broke it off. She's perfectly entitled to keep the ring — and I'd say she has a strong claim to the cat, too.'

'She doesn't care a thing about Cho-Cho and Teddy really loves that cat. She just wants to spite him.'

' "Hell hath no fury . . ." '

Had she been furious enough to consign Cho-Cho to Stuff Yours? Furious enough to bash the taxidermist's head in when he demurred? To set the place on fire? That went beyond fury . . . into madness.

'And you can't get much more scorned than finding your lover has eloped with someone else,' Evangeline continued. 'Cecile says there's been a custody war over the cat ever since. They're forever kidnapping it from each other. The cat doesn't seem particularly bothered, although she favours Teddy.'

'She's such a dear little thing,' I sighed, 'with such a sweet placid temperament.'

'Touch of the geisha there, I'd say. If she were human, that's undoubtedly what she'd be.'

I couldn't deny it. It seemed only too likely. Cho-Cho was a friend to everyone, settling into Eddie's arms as readily as into Soroya's . . . or mine.

'Cheer up!' Evangeline said. 'Look around you and enjoy the scenery.'

We were strolling through the warren of little side streets clustered around the theatre and I have to admit it was my favourite sort of scenery. It was a delight to see so many idiosyncratic shops lining the streets after the boredom of London's borough high streets which chain stores had so colonized that they all looked alike. By tacit consent, we slowed down to window shop.

Antiques lurked enticingly at the back of dusty window displays, jewellery glittered under spotlights, shock and schlock clothing by hopeful young designers draped mannequins and partial body forms in a lot of the shops. A delicatessen/ sandwich shop in the midst of it all probably did a thriving business with all the shopkeepers and their customers. And still the shops stretched on, featuring candles, incense, crystals, New Age accessories, more antiques, more designers, more —

'Viola!' I gasped, halting before a silver-smith's. There, on a black velvet neck form, rested a beautiful silver-and-enamel necklace of delicately pretty violas. The perfect gift for my lovely granddaughter.

'The shop's closed,' Evangeline pointed out. 'We'll have to come back another day.'

'But will we ever find it again?' We

seemed to have taken so many twisting and turning paths that I despaired momentarily. 'Where are we?'

'There's a street name on the corner.' Evangeline started towards it and I followed reluctantly, looking back over my shoulder at the exquisite little trinket. A namesake necklace for my beautiful little Viola. I couldn't bear to lose it.

'Regency Close,' Evangeline announced, squinting up at the sign. Then she stiffened. 'Trixie — do you smell smoke?'

'Sort of.' I lifted my head and inhaled deeply. Smoke, yes, but not a real-and-present-danger sort of smoke. More like a memory of smoke.

Sniffing like bloodhounds, we turned down another narrow street and followed the scent. I was not particularly surprised when we reached the source of it.

'I didn't realize the taxidermist's was so close to the theatre,' I said. We looked at the blackened ruins, little pools of water still marking hollows in the debris.

'We should have known. Cecile has been too busy at the theatre to get around much.' Evangeline's face was grim as she surveyed the scene.

'It must be what gave her that gruesome idea.' I shivered and not just at the thought of a stuffed Fleur. The sun had dropped below the horizon and darkness was swooping over us. Moreover, the wind was rising, chill and relentless. Suddenly I yearned for home — even our temporary home at Matilda's.

'Evangeline,' I began, 'let's —'

'Halt!' A slight quaver in the voice rather undermined the command. 'Who goes there?'

'Goes where?' Evangeline swung around irritably. 'Who the devil are you and what do you think you're playing at?'

'Just what I was going to ask you.' Strangely, Evangeline's burst of temper seemed to reassure our challenger. He stepped forward smartly, with a soldier's gait and still with that faint air of relief. 'What are you doing here?'

'Why shouldn't we be here?' Evangeline wasn't going to let him get away with that. 'And who are you?'

'Perhaps he's the night watchman,' I ventured, as he seemed in no hurry to answer.

'Don't tell me this dump ever ran to a night watchman!' Evangeline snorted. 'Not even in its heyday!'

'True, madam, true,' the old boy agreed. 'Only too true.'

'Then who are you?' Evangeline demanded.

'An interested party. A neighbour. A householder, who doesn't want his property devalued by the presence of ghosts.'

'Ghosts?' I stared at him incredulously. 'You're kidding!'

'A man died in this fire, you know. Gone before his time. That sort can leave a restless spirit behind them.'

'Nonsense!' Evangeline's tone was robust, but I noticed that she moved a little closer to me. My own shiver wasn't entirely due to the icy wind.

'You may think so, but there are those who claim to have seen them. Yes, and just where you're standing.'

'Have you?' she demanded. 'If anything haunted this place, I should think it would be the shades of all those poor benighted animals who were skinned and —'

'Don't!' I saw Cho-Cho's bright trusting face before me and couldn't bear the thought of the fate she had so narrowly escaped. If we hadn't come along . . .

'No,' he said. 'They'd have no reason to remain here. They were peacefully departed before they ever came here. There's no harm from them.'

Were they? Cho-Cho hadn't been.

'Harm?' Evangeline was quick to pick him up on it. 'So, it's not just a simple ghost, it's a malevolent one.'

'Why shouldn't it be, departing like that? If it happened to you, I dare say you'd be back in no time and howling for blood.'

'He's got your number,' I couldn't resist saying.

'No,' he continued, 'it's been quiet, so far. But when I saw the two of you — from a distance, dark shapeless forms, just like him — I thought he'd come back and brought a friend with him.'

'Really?' Evangeline was huffy because of that shapeless remark. 'I've never heard of ghosts in pairs. They're usually alone or, if not, centuries apart and unaware of each other.'

Come to think of it, she was right. Your average ghost isn't really the matey sort. At least, not with his peers, although he might occasionally try to cosy up to the living — when not content merely to scare the living daylights out of them.

'Not always. There are well-documented sightings of entire Roman legions marching along the old roads they built. And then there was the case of —'

'We are not here to discuss ghosts,' Evangeline said frostily.

'The question is: what was the ghost doing here?' I broke in quickly before he asked us what *we* were here for.

'Swooping about, bobbing up and down, pinpoint lights flashing all around him. Sometimes he looked ten feet tall, then he'd sort of retract and become just a bump in the ground.'

'Or a bump in the night,' Evangeline said tartly. 'Were there any sound effects to this appearance or was it all visual?'

'I didn't want to get too close,' he said defensively. 'I kept my distance but, when the wind blew in my direction, there seemed to be a sort of moaning and sobbing.'

'An emotional ghost,' Evangeline sniffed. She didn't believe a word of it.

'You might shed a tear or two if you'd been cut down in your prime.'

'He was a young man, then?' I realized we were in danger of letting irrelevancies spoil an opportunity for gathering first-hand information. 'You knew him? What was he like?'

'I wouldn't say I knew him. He kept himself to himself, but he always spoke pleasantly enough when you saw him. Sightings were fairly rare, though, he was the night owl type. Shop could get pretty lively after dark. Lots of comings and goings, mostly through the back door.'

'Up to no good!' Evangeline deduced instantly.

'I didn't say that.' He stepped back nervously.

'You implied it.' Evangeline advanced on him. 'What do you think he was —'

'You seem to keep a pretty close eye on this place.' I came to a deduction of my own. 'You don't happen to be the one who saw a taxi leaving here on the day of the fire?'

'Nothing . . . No . . .' Unnerved by our concerted attack, he swung around and began to walk away as fast as he could without actually running.

'Well, now we know the busybody who called the police and ratted on Eddie.'

'And he knows us! Your question would have made him suspicious. Any minute he may remember that we were around on that day too, and call the police again.' She glared at me and I glared back.

Nasty looks and recriminations notwithstanding, we were rapidly moving away from the scene.

'Turn here!' Evangeline whirled us around a corner and then another before we began to slow down a bit. 'Up here!' It was only a small hill but we were already panting. The smell of stale smoke had receded, however, and the whole episode was beginning to assume a dreamlike quality.

'Down here!' The territory was becoming more and more familiar. As we turned the final corner, I recognized it.

'The stage door! We've come in a circle. We're back at the Royal Empire!'

'Stuff Yours had to be nearby for Cecile to know about it.' Evangeline nodded. 'She isn't the sort to go out of her way exploring. Unlike you.'

'I like to know where I am, in relation to everything around me.' I couldn't understand people who didn't.

'It's all those gangster films you were in,' Evangeline said severely. 'You're always looking for a quick way out in case of trouble.'

'Nothing wrong with that.' It had come in useful more than once in our immediate past. And she knew it, even if she didn't want to admit it.

'Shall we go in?' Evangeline looked at the stage door.

'Better not. We know our way back from here and, I don't know about you, but I'm tired. I can do without any more histrionics.' Famous last words.

'I'm going back to London first thing in the morning!' Jocasta was hovering in the hallway, pale but determined. She faced us as though she expected opposition to her decision.

'That's not a bad idea,' Evangeline agreed. 'We could do with a quick trip to Town to attend to a few errands ourselves.'

'I only intended to drive you down and go straight back,' Jocasta continued with her obviously rehearsed argument, not noticing that it had become unnecessary.

'And now you can drive us back again. We'll be ready by ten thirty and you can have us there in time for lunch.'

'I was planning to leave around 7 a.m.' It was a rear-guard action and Jocasta knew it.

'Nonsense! You don't want to get caught up in rush-hour traffic. The motorway should be fairly clear by ten thirty.'

'What about Eddie?' I protested. 'We can't go off and leave him here alone.' Especially as he wouldn't be in this mess if it wasn't for us.

'We'll only be away overnight. It isn't as though we're leaving the country.'

She would, if it suited her. At the moment, it didn't. She was up to something, though. I knew that sneaky look on her face of old.

'Ten thirty . . .' Jocasta was still struggling with her own problem. How had her

184

simple plans become so disrupted?

'We'll stop at Hugh's first.' Smoothly, Evangeline continued to rearrange everyone's life. 'You can have your meeting with Martha then and I know Trixie will want to see the children.'

I nodded enthusiastically before I began to wonder, What's wrong with this picture? Then I had it. 'And what will you be doing?'

'Talking to Hugh, for one thing. He's a dear boy, but I'm afraid it's very much out of sight, out of mind, with him. We want to show our faces periodically to remind him that we're still around.'

Somehow, I doubted that he could forget it, but she had a point. It never hurt to flaunt yourselves in front of Management every once in a while.

'London?' The voice soared out from the top of the stairs. 'You're driving to London in the morning? Splendid. I'll be ready. Ten thirty, you say. That will suit my arrangements perfectly. You can drop me off at Trafalgar Square.'

We looked up in time to see Soroya disappearing along the upper landing before anyone could gainsay her.

'But . . .' Jocasta was still struggling to come to terms with the disruption that ensued every time she tried to do something.

She looked from Evangeline to me.

I shrugged, wondering just when Soroya had returned to the fold. Or had she been lurking in her room all this time, like a spider at the centre of a web, listening to the life of the house going on around her?

'What about you?' Jocasta turned to Evangeline desperately. 'Are you going to let that dreadful woman get away with that?'

'Do you want to be the one to tell her she can't come with us?' Evangeline asked innocently.

'No . . .' Jocasta paled at the thought.

'We'll only have to put up with her for an hour or so,' Evangeline soothed, 'depending on how fast you drive. And, who knows, we might learn something.'

Chapter Fourteen

In the event, we learned nothing. We must have broken the speed record — without actually breaking any laws — getting to London in the morning.

Soroya had beaten Evangeline to the punch and was already ensconced in the front passenger seat when we went down to the car. A grim-faced Jocasta stared straight ahead, ignoring our greetings. We had barely seated ourselves when the car shot forward and aimed towards the motorway.

All attempts at conversation had been defeated by Soroya's brusque, 'I can't hear a thing.' Jocasta did not even bother to answer.

'No, no, no!' Soroya protested, as Jocasta tried to pull over to the kerb to let her out when we reached our destination. 'It's not good enough! I want the other side of the Square!'

Jocasta looked at the bumper-to-bumper traffic ahead of us and her shoulders tensed. I waited for the explosion — it was long overdue.

Brrr-brrr . . . *brrr-brrr* . . . Saved by the

bell. Evangeline's mobile sounded abruptly and she fished it out of her bag.

'Hello? . . . Yes . . .' Her eyes narrowed and she handed the phone to me. 'It's for you.'

'Thanks.' I took it meekly. She hates it when someone calls me on her phone, although, really, only one person ever does. And not very often. 'Martha?'

'Mother, I hope I've caught you in time. Don't go to the house, I'm not there. I'm at your flat. I'll wait for you here.'

'Darling, why — ?' But she'd hung up. I braced myself to break the news to Jocasta. Docklands was a long way from where she had thought she was taking us. I wondered how much out of her way it would be. Still, she had to see Martha, anyway.

'Uh . . . Jocasta . . .' I gave the phone back to Evangeline and tried for a tone that was both conciliatory and apologetic without being too much of each. 'I'm afraid there's been a change of plan.'

'Oh?' Her tone was forbidding.

'Martha,' I said firmly. 'That was Martha. She's at the flat in Docklands. We're to meet her there.'

'Docklands?' Soroya settled back triumphantly. 'Then you'll need to cross the Square, anyway.'

★ ★ ★

'Oh, Mother!' Martha looked almost as harried as Jocasta when she opened the door to us. 'I'm sorry to take over your place like this — but everything is in such a mess at home!'

'Darling, we're always glad to have you here.' I ignored Evangeline's snort. Martha's incipient tears were not so easy to ignore.

'What's wrong? The children . . . ?' Another fear shook me. Had something happened to Hugh? Had they split up? 'Hugh . . . ?'

'No, no, they're fine. Hugh sends his love.' Evangeline snorted disbelievingly again. 'The children have gone to the Zoo with the au pair. I couldn't have them underfoot here. Everyone is underfoot at the house — and it's so humiliating!'

'Humiliating?' Irritating, I could understand. Infuriating, certainly. Upsetting, yes, but . . . humiliating?

'Terribly! You know Hugh works mostly from home. He's been having a lot of meetings in his study lately. And I've been trying to test some of the recipes in the kitchen . . .'

'I think I see.' Light was beginning to dawn.

'Well, you know what theatre people are like.'

'Always hungry,' I agreed, 'and when good smells are drifting from the kitchen, they just follow their noses.' We'd all been there.

'Exactly! They just couldn't keep away. Which would have been all right, if I were working from my own recipes. But you never know what's going to result when you try someone else's — that's why we have to test them. Oh!' Tears were close again. 'I'll never forget the look on Sir Feltham's face when he bit into that scone and it was all raw in the middle. And he thought it was my fault!'

'I'm sure he understood when you explained.'

'He said he did, but I'm sure he thought I was just making excuses. He doesn't believe I can cook! I heard him giving Hugh the telephone number of what he called a "superior domestics" agency.'

'Oh, darling!'

'It's those recipes the stars are sending in! Most of them are all wrong!' She rounded on Jocasta as though the poor girl had been personally responsible for each and every one of them. 'None of those idiots know the first thing about cooking! They're bluffing — making everything up!'

'That's why we're testing everything.'

Jocasta stood her ground. 'I know for a fact that some of them are very good cooks, but you have to be careful. When some cooks give you their special recipes, it's a known fact that they often withhold one or two of the ingredients, so that you can't duplicate their results. We'll have to check and double-check everything.'

'Some inspired guesses would help, too,' I suggested. 'They might add ingredients instead of leaving something out.'

Evangeline wandered off, bored by all this domesticity. She was always happy to eat the end result, but she didn't want to know the particulars of achieving it.

The rest of us moved purposefully towards the kitchen. Martha had obviously hurled everything into shopping bags and brought them over here. Now they were strewn across the table and the half-full bags occupied every chair. The place looked as though a whirlwind had struck it and I welcomed the look. It took away the memory I was afraid was waiting for me: a gentle loving little cat who had trustingly allowed me to take her into the car and down to Brighton. We had both thought she would be coming back.

'I wasn't sure what you had here,' Martha said, 'so I just brought everything.'

'So I see.' I had the feeling that she had included things she would need herself at home. I would have to check on that before she left.

'Scales, measuring spoons — everything is different here. Do you realize they have all these different spoons they measure with?' Her voice rose indignantly. 'In between the teaspoon and the tablespoon, they use something called a dessert spoon — which looks like a tablespoon to me, while their tablespoon is more like our serving spoon. And none of them hold the same amount as ours. And the scales — scales! — who ever heard of weighing the dry ingredients instead of measuring them? But the cups are different sizes, too. Nothing is the same! How am I ever going to make sense of all these recipes?'

'That's why I'm here to help you,' Jocasta reminded her.

'Let me make you a cup of tea, dear,' I soothed. 'Don't worry, we'll sort it all out.'

'And as if that wasn't bad enough,' Martha would not be diverted, 'they've gone metric. So you can get Imperial measures, metric measures and something they laughingly call American measures — which aren't right, which makes you doubt all the other measurements.'

The doorbell cut across her jeremiad, but she continued, 'And there are gills and pints and millilitres and centilitres and ounces and grams and —'

'I'll get the door,' I told Jocasta, 'and perhaps you'd better get her something stronger than tea . . .'

'Ah!' Nigel shifted from foot to foot as I opened the door. 'I was expecting . . . that is, I thought . . .'

'You want Evangeline?' I stepped back. 'Come in. I'll go and get her for you.'

'It's just that I have a little something for her. For both of you, actually.'

A loud anguished wail from the kitchen startled us. Nigel looked in that direction and began backing away.

'Ah . . . it appears to be an inopportune moment. Perhaps another time . . .'

'I'm afraid Martha is in the midst of a culinary crisis,' I explained. 'Come along and provide some distraction. It might help.'

'Ah. Yes.' He sidled forward reluctantly. Not, I was sure, because he cared about being helpful, but because he had just seen Evangeline emerge from her room and head towards the kitchen to find out what was going on.

'And now *this* one is in *Australian* mea-

193

sures!' Martha was sitting upright at the table, tense and white-faced, one hand curled around a glass. 'I never should have agreed to do it,' she moaned. 'I had no idea what was involved. We'll never make that deadline.'

'I wanted to give her a glass of white wine,' Jocasta apologized, 'but all I could find was more of that awful brandy.'

Evangeline sniffed. Her private supply had been raided and was now being insulted. She was not best pleased.

'It's all right, it's all right,' I soothed impartially. 'Don't worry, we'll get it all sorted out.'

'Hmmmph!' Evangeline snorted. 'Next thing, you'll say it's always darkest just before the dawn!'

'Well, it is. Usually.' I watched Jocasta tidying the jumbled heap from Martha's kitchen into neat little piles. Round tubs of spices, bottles of flavourings, a long thin cylinder of vanilla pods, another of saffron, squeeze tubes of chili, garlic and anchovy pastes, various herbs, a peppermill, a cheese grater . . .

'Umm, do you really think you need *all* these things, dear?' I ventured. 'I mean, aren't you supposed to be doing recipes for people on the road, going from one engagement to another, never staying long in one place? They won't be carrying a whole kitchen cabinet along with them. They're actors, not professional cooks.'

'Good point,' Evangeline approved. 'One or two little luxury items could be slipped into a suitcase — but not all these.'

'Believe it or not,' Martha said coldly, 'every single one of these ingredients has turned up in one recipe or another. I've had to buy a lot of them especially because of that.'

'Some of the recipes they've donated have been very ambitious,' Jocasta said. Perhaps too much so, her tone implied. 'Adventurous, even.'

'I don't think it's entirely a bad thing,' Martha was beginning to recover, 'for the occasional recipe to call upon them to stretch themselves. We don't want to be too ordinary.'

'Ah!' Nigel stepped forward. 'Perhaps I might make a contribution. I just happen to have brought you a little present . . .' He wriggled his eyebrows meaningfully at Evangeline in a way that would have done credit to Groucho Marx. 'I think you might be able to do something very exciting with it.'

'Oh?' United by sudden mistrust, we all

stared mesmerized at the parcel he held out to us.

'Why, Nigel, how sweet of you.' It was as phoney a reading of a line as Evangeline had ever given. She even simpered as she accepted the parcel — had a small oblong slip of paper passed between them at that moment? — and began unwrapping it.

'What is it?' I asked. I didn't think I was going to like the answer.

'Ostrich steaks!' Nigel said triumphantly. 'The Food of the Future!'

I was right, I didn't like it. And I wasn't alone. Martha drew in her breath sharply; Jocasta simply goggled at Nigel.

'Well!' Evangeline stared down at what she had uncovered. 'It looks very . . . interesting.'

I went over to carry out my own inspection. The meat bore a faint resemblance to chicken, but had a darker colour and a coarser grain.

'And just how are we supposed to cook that?' Martha demanded. 'Do you have a recipe for it?'

'Ah, no. Pretty much like chicken, I suppose. Same family, just a lot bigger. Do you know, just one ostrich egg will make an omelette big enough for ten or eleven —'

'You didn't bring eggs, too?' Martha's voice rose perilously.

'Ah, no . . . but I could get some for you —'

'No, no, this is quite enough,' Jocasta intervened hastily. 'Actually, I seem to recall that one of the supermarket chains tried to launch ostrich meat not so long ago. The instructions on the packet were to cook it very quickly or it might get a bit tough. And I think a sauce was recommended, as it was rather dry.'

'Oh, yes, I remember that!' In fact, it came back to me vividly. A few flagship stores had tried to popularize a whole range of the more exotic meats. The aisle in front of the chill cabinet had been crowded with bemused — not to say stunned — customers staring unbelievingly at the packets labelled Ostrich, Emu, Crocodile, Alligator, Kangaroo, Bear, and the relatively mundane Wild Boar and Venison. Occasionally, one of the braver souls had picked up a package and squinted at the cooking instructions, before carefully replacing it and retreating to the safety of a pound of hamburger. I never saw anyone buy any of it and, presumably, neither did the supermarket, as that particular chill cabinet soon reverted to a display of cold cuts and pâtés.

'That experiment folded faster than an

avant-garde production of *Charlie's Aunt* with everyone in masks and speaking in rhymed couplets.'

'We needn't go into that,' Evangeline said repressively, and, too late, I remembered that she had been inveigled into a production not a million miles away from the one I had so carelessly cited.

'Ah! Well!' Nigel was suddenly shifty-eyed and anxious to get away. 'The world has moved on from that point. Everyone is much more aware of the global market these days . . . the Green Party . . . conserving resources . . . ozone layer . . . global warming . . .' His voice faded as he backed into the hallway and made his escape.

Leaving Evangeline holding the ostrich steaks. We looked at each other and then at her.

'Right!' She thrust them at Jocasta. 'You're the expert. *Do* something with these!'

For a long moment, I thought Jocasta was going to refuse. For a hopeful split-second, I thought she was going to take the package and hurl it at Evangeline's head.

A sudden commotion in the hallway outside distracted us. Raised, apologetic voices, one Nigel's, the other not quite so familiar. The front door slammed and footsteps continued down the hall towards us.

Jocasta accepted the package absently and we all watched the doorway. I'm not sure what we expected, but it was something of an anticlimax when Jasper, our landlord, appeared in the doorway and looked around, blinking.

'Oh, sorry,' he said. 'I didn't realize you had guests.'

'It's just Martha,' I said. 'You remember Martha. And Jocasta, who's helping her with her cookbook.'

'Oh, right.' He nodded to Martha and, more uncertainly, to Jocasta. 'It's just . . . I was hoping for a quick word . . . alone.'

'Come into the drawing room.' I led the way. Evangeline crossed to stand framed by the glass wall with the panorama of the fast-flowing Thames and the old warehouses converted into luxury flats on the other side of the river as her background.

'Now, then,' she demanded, 'what's this all about?'

'Oh, er, nothing, really. I, er, was just wondering . . . Everything all right?'

'Just fine —'

'Why shouldn't it be?' Evangeline and I spoke simultaneously. As I watched Jasper's face, I realized that Evangeline's response was the pertinent one. Something was up, he looked nearly as shifty as Nigel.

'Oh. Oh, no reason. I just thought I'd stop by and make sure everything was satisfactory. You're quite happy here? All things considered?'

'What things?' Evangeline's eyes narrowed.

'Oh, I don't know. Not getting too noisy here, or anything? We've sold almost all the flats now. Business picking up. New people moving in. They're not disturbing you?'

'We've been too busy to notice,' I assured him. It did not seem to be an entirely satisfactory reply.

'Good, good,' he said unconvincingly. 'Er . . . I was wondering. Since you're so happy here, you wouldn't like to buy the flat, would you?'

Evangeline and I looked at each other. Such a thing had never occurred to us.

'Prime location,' he urged. 'Luxury penthouse suite . . . River views . . . Value going up by the minute . . .' He made the mistake of meeting Evangeline's glacial gaze and faltered. 'Er, perhaps you'd like a bit of time to think it over.'

'Unquestionably, we would,' Evangeline said.

'Right! Naturally! Thing is . . . people have been asking about this place. You know . . . Luxury penthouse suite . . .'

'You said that!' Evangeline cut in sharply.

'Er . . . yes . . . right . . .' What was there about us today that was making men shuffle backwards? 'Er . . . I'll leave you to talk it over then . . . give you a good price, of course . . . Er . . . well, goodbye.' He fled from the room.

'You know,' Evangeline looked after him thoughtfully, 'I've had it done with more panache, but I think we've just been given an eviction notice.'

'Put up or shut up,' I agreed. 'Either buy this place or get out.'

'Buy this place . . . ?' Evangeline looked around, still thoughtful.

'It's too far from the centre of things.' I noted the most important drawback. 'Transport links aren't good. If we didn't have Eddie . . .'

'And we don't have Eddie now.' We looked at each other.

'Poor Eddie. I wonder how he's getting on. They can't really enforce that "Don't leave town" order, can they?'

'I don't know any more about police powers here than you do, but I know one thing —' Evangeline straightened up and squared her shoulders — 'Eddie needs us — and we're going to get him out of this mess.'

'Only fair,' I murmured. 'As he keeps reminding us, we got him into it.'

'We're going back to Brighton first thing in the morning,' Evangeline said. 'And this time we'll concentrate on Eddie's plight. That means we'll have to discover who killed Mr Stuff Yours — and why.'

'That might not be so easy. He doesn't sound as though he had a lot of friends who'd be available for questioning.'

'But a lot of people who visited him under cover of night.' Evangeline nodded wisely. 'We'll start with them.'

'How — ?' The full force of her determination struck me like a blow and I changed in mid-question. 'How are the trains in the morning?'

'Trains?' Evangeline's lip curled in distaste. 'Mmm, I don't suppose Jocasta . . . ?'

'I wouldn't suppose it for a moment,' I told her. 'Even if she wasn't thoroughly fed up with us, Martha needs her working here. We don't have any luggage to worry about this time, so I'm afraid it's going to be public transport for us.'

Chapter Fifteen

Two early mornings in a row weren't doing Evangeline's temper any good. I wasn't very happy myself. Only the comforting rattle of the refreshment trolley rolling down the train aisle mollified us.

'We didn't have any breakfast,' she reminded me, as she ordered coffee, muffins, a chicken salad sandwich and, for good measure, added two miniatures of brandy which, I was relieved to see, she tucked into her handbag, murmuring, 'For future reference.'

I duplicated her order, except for the chicken sandwich, and took Scotch instead of brandy. The future reference was bothering me slightly, it was obvious she knew something I didn't know . . . yet.

We took our time leaving the train. Why not? Brighton was the end of the line, we couldn't be carried on to some other station if we were too slow. We let the holiday-makers crowding the aisle disembark ahead of us. I sat there envying them, they looked so happy and carefree. Laughing, juggling holdalls and picnic baskets, calling to their kids, looking forward to a day at the seaside, perhaps even a week or more. They didn't have to worry about things like arson and murder and police restrictions.

Neither did we — at least, not full time. My spirits rose, buoyed up by all the happy anticipation surrounding us. It was another beautiful day, the sea air was invigorating as we stepped from the train and walked down the platform. Overhead, sunlight beamed through the glass roof, throwing latticed shadows in our path. I tried to decide why this feeling of coming home should have suddenly engulfed me.

Perhaps it was because of all the bustle and bubbling life around me, so different from the austere and rather bleak air of Docklands. Oh, Docklands was doing its best, but it was still like one of those places where, when you get there, there's no there there.

Brighton, on the other hand, as someone had once noted, looked like a town that was helping the police with their inquiries. Perhaps it was slightly shady, but one felt Life's rich cornucopia was overflowing here.

We walked out on to the station forecourt, looked past the waiting buses at the low hill leading down to the big shops and the seafront. Smaller shops stretched along each side of the hill, full of souvenirs and tat. Over all was the faint smell of fish and chips and, everywhere, people, people, people.

'This,' Evangeline said, 'is more like it!' We beamed at each other. It was our kind of place.

'We don't have to go straight back to Matilda's, do we?' I pleaded. 'Not right away?'

'Well . . .' Evangeline pretended reluctance, but I could see that the dizzying devil-may-care atmosphere was getting to her. 'I suppose we can't really do anything until later, anyway. And we've never seen the Royal Pavilion.'

'Oh, yes! I'd love to see the Royal Pavilion! It's supposed to be fabulous — all that chinoiserie! And the Lanes! I want to explore the Lanes in daylight. With the shops all open, so that we can actually go in and buy something!'

'Missing your retail therapy, are you?' But she was as excited by the idea as I was. We were just beginning to realize how cut off we had been in Docklands, where it was such a long haul to the West End and back. And when we got back . . .

I began to feel more kindly disposed towards Jasper. It was no great tragedy to be evicted from the middle of nowhere. If he could make a healthy profit from his luxury penthouse, why not? We could find a lot livelier places to live. Practically anywhere else, for instance.

Even here. I looked around with fresh interest, trying to picture it at its worst on a bleak and wet and cold winter's day out of season, without all the crowds and colour. Even so, it had a lot more to recommend it than our current stamping grounds. Theatres, cinemas, cabaret venues, places of historical interest, restaurants, cafés, and shops of all sorts and descriptions — quite unlike the boring regulation high street monoliths that were beginning to invade Docklands under the guise of offering consumer goods that people were supposed to want.

Oh, yes, this was more like it. We meandered along the Lanes, zigzagging from side to side to window shop, price, compare, decide we weren't really interested and move along to the next enticing display window.

'Interesting, but not interesting enough.' Evangeline turned away from the glittering array of jewels.

I agreed. That little silver-and-enamel necklace of violas was shining like a beacon in my memory. It was nicer than anything we had seen so far and quite,

quite perfect for Viola. I must go back and get it as soon as possible before — oh, horrible thought! — someone else fell for it and bought it first.

Still lost in the pleasant dream of Viola opening her birthday present and squealing with delight, it took me several moments to realize what I was looking at when we stopped in front of the next shop.

Cats! Cats everywhere. Cats in pictures, in pewter, in china, in porcelain, in carved quartz, in every possible combination and variation of the beautiful, the cutesy, the twee, the dignified and the utterly revolting. And everything a cat might desire, from climbing posts to cushioned beds, from catnip mice to munchies, to balls, toys — Oh, and Cho-Cho would just love that little —

To my horror, I found myself bursting into tears. I didn't have Cho-Cho. I didn't have a cat at all.

'Oh, for heaven's sake!' Exasperated, Evangeline grabbed my arm and yanked me away from the window. 'Pull yourself together! We have too much to do tonight for you to go to pieces now!'

'I'm trying,' I sniffed, 'but —' The import of her words got through to me. I'd known she was up to something. 'What too much? What are we doing tonight?'

★ ★ ★

It got cold when the sun went down — and the sun had been down for a long time. Even the moon was thinking of quitting. A chill wind swept from off the water, the smell of wet ashes was beginning to turn my stomach.

'Evangeline —' I was tired and frozen and fed up. 'How much longer do we have to hang around here?'

'How do I know how long it will take?' Evangeline pulled her cloak tighter around her and tried to pretend she wasn't shivering. 'Stop whining.'

'I'm not whining. I merely asked a simple question. And I've got another: suppose he doesn't show?'

'Then we'll try again tomorrow night.'

That was what I was afraid of. 'He might not come at all. He might have already found whatever he was looking for. If it was anybody looking for anything at all — that's only your theory.'

'There must be something to be found. Otherwise, he wouldn't have set fire to the place. Arson is always used to destroy the evidence.'

'Not always. Sometimes it's done as an insurance fraud.' We both spoke from the depths of experience our B-movie scripts had given us. I had the uneasy feeling that

I wouldn't like to take either theory to Superintendent Thursby and try to convince him of it.

Even more uneasily, I recalled the state of that back office just before the fire erupted. I had thought Mr Stuff Yours was just another untidy slob, but it was possible that Evangeline was right and someone had been rootling through the files and paperwork searching for incriminating evidence.

'Anyway, for whatever reason, he made a pretty good job of destruction.' I looked into the ruins the wavering moonlight revealed: the charred lumps half-hidden in the heaps of ashes strewn across what had once been the floor, the blackened hulks of the bits of wall still standing, the jagged shards of the showroom window. 'There can't be anything left to be found.'

'Then why should someone keep returning under cover of darkness?'

'Maybe a hopeful looter? Or, perhaps . . . I don't suppose you'd care to consider the possibility that the old boy the other night was right and it really is a ghost?'

'Believe that and you're as crazy as he is! No, there's still something here that someone wants desperately — and he'll keep coming back until he finds it.'

'Maybe.' She could be right. I hoped she

wasn't. If she was, it was very silly of us to have come here by ourselves to face the villain. We tended to overlook the fact that, when we were tiptoeing through the perils in our films, we had a camera crew, stunt people for the dangerous bits and a director to yell 'Cut!' when the action got too hairy. Now we were acting out the scripts all on our own — with no cavalry to ride to the rescue if we got into trouble.

At the very least, we should have brought Eddie with us. It was his neck we were trying to save, after all.

Why hadn't I thought of that before? 'Too soon old, too late schmart,' as the saying went. If Evangeline tried to drag me over here tomorrow night, I would definitely drag Eddie along —

'What's that?' A dark shape was materializing at the far edge of the ruins, seeming to float above them. Maybe Eddie wouldn't have been so useful, at that. A silver bullet, perhaps, or a —

'Our quarry!' Evangeline was triumphant. 'Be quiet — and watch!'

'*Uuuuh-hoooo . . . uuuh-hoooo . . .*' The sobbing, shuddering moans made the hair prickle at the back of my neck as the figure glided closer.

Suddenly, the night became even darker.

Dimly, I realized that lights had been snapped off behind several previously glowing windows near us — as though their brightness might attract the attention of any roving demons.

'*Uuuuh-hooooo . . .*' The figure glided and swooped, swerved and dipped, in some macabre dance of its own devising, approaching ever nearer. The ashes, disturbed every time it swooped, flurried into the air and were swirled across the debris by the wind.

My throat began to ache from the fine ash dust and I found I was afraid to clear it. I didn't want to attract any attention, either.

The figure stretched up so high it seemed to blot out the watery moon, then contracted and slithered along at ground level, bobbing up and down unevenly.

Wasn't there some legendary phantom called the Shape-Shifter? Was that what we had here? But wasn't this the wrong part of the world for it? I tried to remember which culture had given rise to that particular revenant. Was it Oriental? Asian? Native American?

Whatever it was, it was getting closer. I found myself backing away. Evangeline wasn't exactly standing her ground, either. In fact, we were bumping against each other in our haste to put more space between ourselves and the encroaching shape.

'*Eeeee-aaaah* . . .' With an agonized howl, the thing hurled itself lengthwise on top of an ash heap and began scrabbling at it. Clouds of ash sprayed into the air and the wind carried it in our direction.

I held my breath.

The figure was twisting and bobbing. If it were human, I would have said it seemed to be tugging at something. With a final gasp of exertion and another explosion of ashes, it pulled that something free and raised it aloft, wailing. The wind gusted and more ashes swirled around us.

I couldn't help it, I coughed.

The dark figure stiffened and turned towards us. Its thin reedy hiss seemed an echo from another world. 'Who'sss there? Whooo isss it?'

Was I imagining it, or was there something vaguely familiar in the tonal quality underlying those sibilants? Evangeline had no doubt.

'Cecile!' Evangeline strode forward briskly. 'What the devil are you playing at?'

'Fleur . . .' Dame Cecile moaned. 'My darling Fleur . . . I have nothing of her now . . . nothing! And we're opening tomorrow night — I can't bear it! For nearly twenty years, my little darling sat in the chair beside my dressing table, watching over me as I applied my make-up. I don't know how I can go on without her! But if I can't have her dear little body curled up in the chair, then I want her ashes in a box on the mantelpiece. It's my right!'

'There are nothing but ashes here,' Evangeline said. 'How do you expect to separate hers from the rest?'

'I've found them! They're here! Where I found her dear little spine!' Dame Cecile threw out one hand dramatically. From it dangled an improbably long chain of jointed bones. Evangeline and I exchanged sceptical glances.

'But the little mutt was — er, I mean, Fleur was a Pekinese,' Evangeline pointed out. 'Not a dachshund.'

'You may sneer, if you like,' Dame Cecile said. 'But I think — I *know!* — this is my dear little Fleur!'

There was something lumpy in the ashes at my feet. Absently, I stirred them with a toe, then wished I hadn't. They fell away to reveal a large claw. I remembered the golden eagle that had hung from the ceiling. And then I remembered what had been coiled in a nearby corner.

'Think again, Cecile,' I said. 'I'll give you odds that's the remains of the hooded cobra.'

Chapter Sixteen

Having poured the contents of our miniatures down Dame Cecile's gullet before we
could persuade her to move, we took the
precaution of stopping at the all-night off-
licence for fresh supplies on the way back to
Matilda's.

At which point, Dame Cecile had an attack of hauteur, shook away our supporting arms and insisted that she was
quite capable of climbing the stairs by herself. Not only that, she wanted to be alone.

We stood uneasily at the foot of the
stairs and watched her weave her way up,
prepared to do our best to catch her if she
fell. It was just as well that she didn't; it
had been a long day and our best wouldn't
have been very good.

'Was that Soroya?' Matilda appeared at
the top of the stairs.

'No, it was Cecile,' Evangeline answered.

'Where's Soroya?'

'Who knows?' I shrugged.

'Who cares?' Evangeline went one better
— and truer.

'I don't care. Not about her.' Matilda descended the stairs slowly. 'But I don't like to go to bed while she's still out. I know — only too well! — that she has her own key, but she never bothers to lock the door behind her. I want to know that the house is secure for the night when I go to bed.'

'Quite right,' Evangeline approved, stifling a yawn.

'What time is it? I'm afraid I dozed off.'

'Ummm . . .' We exchanged glances, tossing a mental coin. I lost. 'It, um, seems to be about one thirty.'

'One thirty? And Cecile is just getting in!' She stopped, seemed to listen to herself, then gave a self-deprecating little laugh. 'Sorry, I didn't mean to sound like an outraged parent, but Cecile must realize we're opening tomorrow — tonight. What is she doing running around until this hour?'

We didn't even exchange glances on that one. Neither of us was going to do any explaining.

'Both of them —' Matilda continued her plaint — 'Cecile and Soroya — in and out. Out until all hours. And not together. Oh, no, that would be too simple. I'm forever waiting up for one or the other. Believe me, house guests are hell!

'Oh, er, present company excepted, of

course. I didn't mean you . . .' She let the valiant lie trail off. It was one thirty in the morning and we had just come in, too.

At least we'd brought Cecile with us. We ought to get Brownie points for that.

'Lock up and go back to bed.' Evangeline did not bother to stifle her yawn this time. 'Soroya won't be back now. The last we saw of her, she was in Trafalgar Square, prepared to go off and make someone else's life miserable. With any luck, they've killed her.'

I wish Evangeline wouldn't joke about things like that. It was too close to home.

'Matilda may complain about her house guests —' it was still rankling with Evangeline — 'but she doesn't have such great luck with her housekeepers, either.'

'You can say that again!' We were in my room, having voted ourselves a nightcap, since we were exhausted and chilled to the bone from our long vigil. 'What *did* happen to the last housekeeper — the one before that poor Australian woman in the cellar? Do you know if she left of her own free will? I mean —'

'Or was she pushed, you mean.' Evangeline poured another drink. 'I understand she left in the time-honoured way.

Flouncing out in a towering fury for reasons best known to herself.'

'Leaving Matilda in the lurch.' We'd all been there — especially Evangeline. Brooding into my glass, I found that the brandy had started up several disquieting thoughts and was chasing them around my head. Or had they been there all along?

'Evangeline, do you think maybe Eddie could be right and those stairs were deliberately booby-trapped? Suppose the trap had been set for the last housekeeper and not the poor soul who got caught in it?'

'I was wondering how long it would take you to get around to that.' Her tone was maddeningly superior.

'Oh? And you were there ahead of me?'

'Way ahead. Who'd bother to kill a housekeeper? And why? It's far more likely that any trap was set for Matilda herself.'

'On the cellar stairs? She barely knew where they were.'

'It wouldn't have been hard to find an excuse to send her to them.'

'Who'd want to kill Matilda? Now, if someone wanted to kill Soroya, I could understand it. Yes,' I found myself warming to the idea, 'anyone might have wanted to kill Soroya.'

'Including Matilda.' Evangeline stopped

me cold with that one.

'No! I can't believe Matilda as a murderess!'

'It would solve a lot of her problems if she got rid of Soroya . . . permanently.'

'Look at it the other way: it would solve Soroya's problem if she got rid of Matilda.'

'Soroya doesn't have a problem, she knows when she's well off. She may carp, but it suits her to have Matilda in residence, taking care of the property — and paying the taxes.'

'It's Matilda's house.' I wasn't going to carry on with that argument, a better suspect had occurred to me. 'Anyway, how about Teddy? I'll bet he'd love to get rid of Soroya. If only to have a peaceful life and not have to keep snatching back his own cat.'

'I'm not so sure about that.' A distant look came into Evangeline's eyes. 'Then, again, we mustn't overlook Cecile. She's very temperamental and has been through an emotional time lately. When passions run high, there's no telling what might happen.'

'Cecile?' I gasped with horror, unable to believe that Evangeline was so cold-bloodedly considering one of her oldest and dearest friends as a possible murderess. 'That's ridiculous! There's nothing in the world that could turn Dame Cecile into a killer.'

'Isn't there?' Evangeline raised an eyebrow at me. 'What if Matilda — even by accident — had done something to harm Fleur? Perhaps even hasten her demise? Do you think Cecile would let her get away with that? Oh, no, she'd want revenge, blood for blood —'

'You've had enough!' It wasn't easy, but I wrested the glass from her hand and hauled her to her feet. The remaining liquid sloshed on to the carpet. 'Go and sleep it off!'

'Just think it over.' Evangeline headed for the door with exaggerated dignity.

Just then a floorboard creaked outside the door. Someone was out in the hallway. Had they been listening at the door? Whoever they were, they would have heard no good of themselves. Serve them right.

'Through the bathroom . . .' Just the same, I didn't want Evangeline to run into them. 'And don't make any noise.'

No one missed Soroya in the morning. She still wasn't around, but no one missed her. They were too caught up in their own worries.

'I can't remember a word!' Dame Cecile kept repeating what seemed to be her mantra. 'Not one word!'

'You'll be all right once the curtain goes up.' Matilda attempted to comfort her. 'And Frella will be in the prompt corner. She'll see you through.'

'Frella hates me!' Dame Cecile declared. 'She hates you, too, because you're harbouring Soroya. She'd be delighted to see us both fall flat on our faces — if only it wouldn't reflect badly on her direction.'

'You don't mean that,' Matilda said, not very convincingly. 'Frella is hard-working and ambitious. She wouldn't want anything to happen to jeopardize the show — it's her big chance.'

'That's what I just said! But she'd have a better chance if she got rid of Teddy.' Dame Cecile was severe in judgement. 'He's undermining the whole production.'

'She'd rather get rid of all of us first,' Matilda sighed.

'She's besotted with that man.'

'I suppose he is charming — in his way,' Cecile conceded. 'I just wish he were more competent.'

'He's not really incompetent,' Matilda said, 'just a lazy actor. Frella lets him get away with too much.'

'She seemed to be tightening the reins yesterday,' I commented.

'Too little, too late.' Matilda shook her

head sadly. 'She'll never get him into shape for tonight.'

'*Well!*' Dame Cecile exclaimed triumphantly.

We all turned to her expectantly. She beamed at us.

'Well what?' Evangeline prodded.

'*Well!* That's my first word. I've got it! *Well!*'

'Congratulations.' Evangeline turned away, losing interest. 'Now all you need are the other few-thousand-odd.'

'It's a start,' Matilda defended, staunchly looking on the bright side.

A sudden burst of hammering shattered the momentary peace and shook the inner wall.

'How can I be expected to remember my lines with all that racket?' Dame Cecile shrieked. 'Make him stop!'

'He's so enthusiastic,' Matilda murmured. 'I don't like to discourage him.'

Having repaired the cellar stairs to the admiration of all, Eddie now had the bit in his teeth and was swooping through the house looking for other jobs to do.

'He's going to fix that wobbly shelf in the closet in my room,' I said. 'It desperately needs doing. The clothing rail is suspended from it and every time I hang something up, I'm afraid it will come down on my head.'

'He's promised to build a set of bookshelves in my bedroom,' Matilda said. 'I think that's what he's working on now. I really need them. I was so pleased when he offered to do it.'

'So-o-o . . .' Dame Cecile's eyes narrowed and she looked to Evangeline for reinforcements. 'I'm surprised your poor head hasn't started to ache with all this noise. You were always so sensitive to such things.'

'We'll be leaving for the theatre soon.' It was a good try, but Evangeline wasn't going to lead the cavalry to the rescue. Too bad Teddy wasn't here to oblige.

'Besides,' Evangeline added, 'there are a couple of loose floorboards in my room that are driving me mad. They not only creak like a door in a Hammer film, but I'm afraid my foot will go through them if I don't tread carefully.'

'These old houses,' Matilda sighed. 'They're lovely to look at, but there's always something that needs repairing every time you turn around.'

As though on cue, there came more enthusiastic hammering. Not only that, but Eddie began to whistle loudly. At least he was happy.

'I'm leaving now!' Outnumbered, Dame Cecile abandoned the battle and prepared to flee the field. 'Perhaps I can find some peace and quiet in my dressing room!' She stalked away and the slam of the front door was louder than the hammer blows.

'Bad dress rehearsal, good opening.' The cast were consoling themselves with the old theatrical cliché.

For myself, I wouldn't like to bet on it. However much Frella had worked on him, Teddy was still flattening everything. And, with a foolproof, actorproof script like *Arsenic and Old Lace*, that was saying something.

Perhaps Frella had leaned on him too much. 'Cowed' was now the word when it came to Teddy. Which was not what the hero of San Juan Hill and subsequent President of the United States had ever been.

This Teddy would not have led an army charging up San Juan Hill, he would have crept up quietly by himself (who would have followed him?), occasionally calling out tentatively, 'I say, you chaps, can't we talk this over?'

'Desperate times,' Evangeline said grimly, 'call for desperate measures.'

'You mean, like cancelling the show?' It

was the only measure I could think of that would save Dame Cecile and Matilda from being damned by association with a major flop.

'Never!' Evangeline turned away abruptly. 'I must confer with Cecile!'

'Good luck!' I'd had enough. 'I'm going out for a breath of air.'

Outside it was cold and dank and starting to rain. I changed my mind, but not to the extent of joining Evangeline in her conference with Cecile. I decided to find a quiet corner backstage and lose myself there until the opening.

It was unnerving to walk along the narrow corridor and hear the sounds emanating from the cast dressing rooms on both sides. The sobs were the worst. A disjointed phrase or sentence was nearly as bad. '. . . pay the mortgage' . . . 'school fees' . . . 'decent holiday for once' . . . 'overdraft' . . .

The usual epidemic of First Night Nerves was rampaging backstage, fuelled by Teddy's ineptness. Or should it be Frella who was blamed? Nepotism was all very well — and sometimes it even worked. But this was one of the times when it didn't.

I tried to tell myself that someone who cared so much for Cho-Cho-San couldn't be all bad — and he wasn't. Not bad —

only . . . useless . . . inadequate . . . out of his depth. 'What ho! Anyone for tennis?' was just about his level. Unfortunately, the part required rather more than that.

A bend in the corridor and a flight of stairs carried me above the miasma of misery that pervaded the dressing-room floor and on to an upper storey where the atmosphere seemed lighter. Perhaps because I couldn't hear all the sounds of pre-opening hysteria.

Somewhere in the distance the faint strains of a violin called invitingly. I followed the melody up a short staircase, around a bend in the narrow hallway, to the open door of a softly lit book-lined room. It was a blissfully domestic scene, in stark contrast to the chaos on the lower floors.

Jem sat in a large armchair beside a glowing fire. Garrick was sprawled lazily across his lap, unconcerned by the notepad propped against his back as Jem scribbled busily. A low side table held a decanter and half-filled glass and two plates, the larger of which contained an assortment of crackers and a chunk of pâté. The smaller just had some rather mauled pâté and a well-licked dollop of what looked like clotted cream. As I watched, Garrick stretched his neck and took another dainty nibble from his share of the pâté.

'Dear lady!' Jem looked up and caught me. 'Do come in. Forgive me for not rising, but . . .' He indicated the large furry reason for his discourtesy. Garrick blinked at me complacently, his trodden tail obviously forgiven and forgotten.

'That's all right, don't disturb him. I was just exploring and stumbled over you. I didn't mean to intrude.'

'No intrusion, all are welcome to my little eyrie. Many an orphan of the storm has sought refuge here. Allow me to offer you a glass of sherry. Or perhaps some claret, or —' his voice deepened into a parody of seduction — ' "Have some Madeira, m'dear?" If —' he reverted to his normal tone — 'you wouldn't mind fetching your own glass?' He waved towards a glass-fronted cabinet in the corner.

I found a wine glass amongst the display of snuff boxes and netsuke. As I turned back, I saw Jem furtively slide the notepad down between the arm of the chair and the seat. I don't know why he was being secretive about it, I had no interest at all in his correspondence.

'This is so pleasant,' I sighed, sinking into the other armchair opposite him.

'Almost civilized,' he agreed. 'Once the

opening is over, life will settle down and it should be more peaceful around here.'

'It's certainly hectic right now.' The sherry was superb. I looked at Jem with new respect — and a certain amount of curiosity. He hadn't picked this up in his local supermarket. Quite a connoisseur, our Jem.

'Jem . . .' The thought followed naturally. 'Jem, my daughter has been landed with editing a theatrical cookbook. A collection of recipes for one person, quick and easy for actors on the move to cook up for themselves in their digs after the show. I don't suppose you have a tasty recipe or two you might like to contribute, do you?'

'Hmm, yes, let me think about that for a bit and see what I can come up with. I haven't toured for years — no, let's be honest, decades. Things are different these days. The old theatrical digs aren't what they used to be. The old landladies have gone, too — which is probably all to the good. They were famous for a lot of things — but cooking wasn't high on the list.'

'Pretty bad, huh?'

'Excruciating!' He winced at the memory. 'Imagine coming back after a performance to find three limp lettuce leaves, two mushy quarters of tomato and a dried-out curling slice of salami with, if you were especially unlucky, a few cubes of beetroot. And bottled salad cream ready to be poured over all. That was quaintly known as "a cold collation". They always had the most grandiose names for the most abysmal offerings.'

'That sounds like a recipe we can do without!'

'And then there were the winter nights when you got a "hot meal" before taking off for the theatre. Meat pie, with a two-inch crust and a thin layer of gristle and gravy; cabbage, simmered down into a green sludge; potatoes, boiled into transparency and disintegrating; and whatever else had been going cheaply at the market stalls that day that you neither could, nor wanted to, identify.'

I shuddered. 'It makes our endless hamburgers and french fries sound epicurean.'

'There's a story,' he reminisced, 'about a young actor who cracked. He'd been on tour for months, each set of lodgings worse than the last, the meals increasingly inedible. He got to the final lodgings and the cooking was so bad he couldn't believe it.

'So he went out and bought himself a thick juicy steak and brought it back to his landlady. "Now listen carefully," he told her. "I want you to put this under a hot grill for three minutes on each side." She nodded. "Then I want you to boil it for half an hour, then put it in the oven and bake it for an hour. Finally, I want you to fry it for fifteen minutes on each side. Now, will you do that for me?" "You can depend on me," she said. "I'll do everything you told me to, I'll follow your instructions exactly." "Yesss," he hissed, snatching it back, "I *thought* you would!" '

Our laughter and Jem's quaking lap unsettled Garrick, who jumped down and ran off.

'It's all right, old boy,' Jem called after him. 'We weren't laughing at you.'

'Oh, dear,' I said. 'I hope he isn't upset.'

'Not at all,' Jem said. 'He's had his nibble and tipple.' Sure enough, the smaller plate was empty. 'It's time for him to go back on duty.' He rose. 'Time for both of us to do our rounds.'

'Thank you for a pleasant interlude,' I said, as we started back for the main body of the theatre.

'My pleasure,' he said. 'Remember, you're welcome up here any time. Anyone is.'

But I noticed he locked the door behind him.

Chapter Seventeen

There was a rustle of anticipation as the curtain went up, then a burst of applause for Matilda, presiding at the tea table, and the two actors flanking her. They froze until the applause subsided and the audience settled back with a happy sigh, prepared to be entertained, but not offended. Given the age of the play, they knew there would be no obscenities, nudity or gratuitous violence; just serial murder, gentle madness and threatened menace. All good clean fun.

Another burst of applause halted the action on Dame Cecile's appearance. Again the actors froze until the enthusiasm had died down and the action could move forward.

Teddy was doing slightly better than walking through his part, but not much. Either Frella's extra coaching hadn't really 'taken' or he'd used so much energy in rehearsal he was now exhausted for the actual performance. I noticed Dame Cecile moving closer to him, as though to point this out in a whisper.

Beside me, Evangeline tensed and leaned forward slightly.

Teddy laid a lackadaisical hand on the stair-rail and lifted one foot as though it were slightly too heavy for him. Dame Cecile sidled a little closer.

'Cha-AAARGE!' Teddy bellowed suddenly, and galloped up the staircase. Even the other actors jumped. Teddy delivered his final line with vehemence and exited, slamming the door behind him so hard he nearly brought the set down. It got the scheduled laugh and another burst of applause.

After a moment of stunned silence onstage, the dialogue began again and the laughs kept coming. Evangeline leaned back in her seat and seemed to breathe more easily.

'All right,' I muttered to a far-too-smug Evangeline, 'what did you do?'

'Nothing, actually,' Evangeline murmured. 'I merely reminded Cecile of the happy days when women wore hatpins. They used to solve so many little difficulties. Cecile can take a hint.'

The crush in the bar during the interval was abuzz with the excitement that presages a major triumph. This show would run and run; in the West End and then on a prolonged tour. But the Royal Empire had it first and self-congratulation was the order of the audience's evening.

'Champagne is called for, I think!'

We hadn't called for it, but we looked approvingly at the opened bottle that had been thrust between us. Our enthusiasm faded a bit when we realized that the arm holding it belonged to Superintendent Thursby.

'A veritable triumph!' he exclaimed. 'All that would have improved it would have been for you two to be in the leading roles.' He brandished the three champagne flutes in his hand. 'Shall I be Mother?'

I hoped his excessive coyness meant that he was off duty, but I didn't much care. The chilled champagne was already flowing into our glasses and it was a great improvement on trying to push our way through the crowd at the bar and get someone to take our order.

'We were offered the parts, of course.' Evangeline didn't specify that the offer had come from a rival management in a different production. 'But we're having an original script written especially for us and we didn't want to tie ourselves down in case of a long run.'

'Very wise.' Thursby gave a vulpine smile which didn't quite reach his watchful eyes. I felt a tremor of disquiet. ('What big teeth you have, Grandmother.') 'With you in the show, it would run for ever. But how interesting to hear that you're going to be in something completely new!' His ears seemed to quiver. 'May one ask what it's about?'

'Now, now!' Evangeline could be coy, too. She waggled a reproving finger at him. 'You must let us keep our little secret for a while longer. Surprise is everything with a new show, you know.' Which was as neat a way as any of concealing the fact that we hadn't a clue what it was going to be about.

'Oh, I know, I know. I do so agree.' They were both overdoing it. All this phoney charm and matiness was making me queasy. 'I'm honoured that you've told me this much.' He splashed more champagne into our glasses. 'There hasn't been a whisper of it on the grapevine yet.'

With good reason. So far, there was nothing to whisper about. In fact, I was becoming increasingly uneasy. It seemed like a long time since we had heard a peep from either the playwright or his enterprising girlfriend.

'Actually, you're the first one we've told — and you have rather tricked us into telling you.'

'Oh, no, not really!' He simpered at her. I hadn't seen such performances since the runners-up had to pretend to be good losers at the Academy Awards.

'Oh, yes. Naughty boy!' Evangeline leaned forward, fluttering her eyelashes. If she'd had a fan, she'd have tapped him with it. '*Very* naughty boy!'

I stopped paying attention. In the distance, over her shoulder, I saw Eddie emerge from the staircase leading to the balcony. He started towards us, then saw who was with us. In one blink of my eyes, he disappeared. One moment he was there; the next, no trace of him.

While I had every sympathy with his reaction, the swift smoothness of it unnerved me. It told me this was not the first time he had done the *Gone in a puff of smoke* act.

Immediately, I wished I hadn't thought of it in quite those terms. My throat closed against the memory of rolling thick smoke; my eyes tried to blink away the flames that flickered, then burst into a raging firestorm; the panic caught at me again and I looked about wildly for escape.

Flashback. It was only a flashback. *Only!*

My pounding heart tried to resume its proper beat. There was nothing to harm me here, nothing to threaten me.

The brightness against my closed eyelids came from the electric lights surrounding the mirrored bar. The noise was the hubbub of the theatre audience gossiping and laughing. The crackling sounds were not made by devouring flames, but by thoughtful people unwrapping their boxes of sweets here rather than in the auditorium after the second act had started.

I tried to take a deep soothing breath — and choked.

'Trixie, are you all right?'

Saved by the bell. It rang out loud and clear, summoning us back to our seats. The first interval had ended, the show was going on.

'Perhaps a bit more champagne at the next interval?' Superintendent Thursby suggested.

'Perhaps not,' Evangeline said. 'There are people we must speak to, but why don't you join us for the party after the show?'

'I'd love to!' His eyes lit up, but there was still a calculating glint in them. I wondered if this was what he had been angling for all along, with his bottle of champagne for bait. Flattery would get him anywhere with Evangeline, but I increasingly distrusted all this sociability.

The second warning bell sounded, brooking no more dawdling. We obediently filed back to our seats.

After the 'Bravos' and the standing ovation, it seemed as though the entire audience had surged backstage, crowding into the dressing rooms, overflowing into the narrow passageway. Voices were too shrill, laughter too loud, elation was punctuated by the popping of champagne corks, but it was the intoxication of success that had gone to everyone's head.

The stagehands were setting up the trestle tables on the stage and food would soon be available. There was breathing space in the wings and I sipped my champagne and watched the caterers. Perhaps they would be serving something Martha might want to know about.

Salads seemed to be the main offering, or perhaps it was just easier to set them out first. A flicker of movement at the base of one of the table legs focused my attention on Garrick, stealthily demolishing a tiny hardboiled egg. I looked up at the table and located a bowl brimming with quails' eggs, beside which huddled smaller bowls containing sea salt flakes, salsa dip and several other strangely coloured dips I couldn't identify.

As I frowned at them, a tiny paw snaked out from behind a floral display and groped towards the quails' eggs.

Greedy Garrick, I thought, then realized that Garrick was still on the floor, gulping the last shreds of his booty. Apart from which, not one of his paws was white.

'Cho-Cho!' I squealed with delight, unfortunately just as one of her claws hooked into a tasty egg. Her paw jerked back, the egg went flying, hitting the edge of the table and rolling on to the floor where Garrick pounced on it rapturously.

A little head emerged from behind the roses and gave me an accusing look.

'I'm sorry, darling,' I said, 'but I was so glad to see you. Here, have another . . .' I selected a plump one and rolled it towards her. She fell on it so eagerly that I wondered when she had last been fed and what they had fed her.

'*Do* you mind . . . ?' an indignant voice said behind me.

I sidestepped to allow a young man carrying a tray of sliced ham and turkey access to the table. He stepped back.

'Take that cat off the table before I set

the tray down,' he ordered. 'I can't tell you the trouble we'd be in if anyone were to see that. There *are* hygiene laws, you know.'

'Really?' You couldn't prove it by me. Judging from some of the sights I'd seen since I arrived in England, I was amazed to know that anyone had ever heard of the word hygiene. There had been the local bakery, where unwrapped cakes were left in the window overnight and late-night passers-by had been able to watch the flies crawling over them. (In response to a complaint, the cakes hadn't been removed, the shades had been pulled down so that you couldn't see what was happening.) And in the late summer, wasps buzzed lazily around fruit displays and over meat in the butcher shops. No one ever seemed bothered about it, least of all the proprietors.

'Really!' He stood there regarding me sternly, waiting.

'Sorry.' I set down my glass and scooped up Cho-Cho, who had finished her egg and was looking at me hopefully, unlike the caterer, who was now scowling. I smiled sweetly at him and helped myself to the largest slice of turkey on his tray. 'This looks so good.'

'Mmmm.' He glowered some more, knowing perfectly well that it was going to slide down the gullet of my furry little friend, who had begun purring loud approval of my action. Garrick too, had begun watching me with interest.

'Bloody animals!' It was muttered low enough for him to deny it if I responded. I didn't. I just smiled sweetly at him and took another slice of turkey as soon as he turned away to go and fetch more food. I dropped the second slice by the table leg for Garrick, but hand-fed Cho-Cho hers. Garrick didn't mind, he wasn't standing on formality when food was concerned.

I crossed the stage to check out the wings on the other side. I was looking for Eddie, hoping he hadn't been too upset at discovering the enemy — otherwise known to him as Superintendent Thursby — in our midst. It wouldn't be a bad idea if he could bring himself to make friends with Thursby and get him on his side. I wondered if that was what Evangeline had had in mind when issuing her invitation.

The supporting players and their friends were having a whoop-de-do on that side, although there was rather more interest in the progress of the buffet than there was on the star side.

There was no sign of Eddie. It wasn't like him to miss a party. I hoped he wasn't too upset. I didn't like to think of him sitting in his lonely room, nursing a beer and a grievance.

Cho-Cho nuzzled my hand and licked up the last shreds of turkey. She looked up at me and craned her neck to look back at the buffet, nearly as interested as the actors. I turned and saw the caterer, followed by two minions, bearing chafing dishes containing the hot food. Beef Stroganoff and creamed chicken, I seemed to recall from a discussion I had overheard at some point.

Something brushed against my ankles and I looked down to find Garrick fondly rubbing against me. Evidently I had replaced Jem temporarily in his affections, since Jem had to be on duty at the stage door and I had free access to the food supplies. Cho-Cho nuzzled my chin, reminding me that she had first claim on my benevolence.

I stroked her absently, still looking around uneasily. Where was Eddie? I wanted to see Eddie.

People were beginning to converge on the buffet now. I saw Superintendent Thursby who, by some sleight of hand, was managing to escort both Evangeline and Dame Cecile. Behind them, Teddy also had a lady on each arm: Matilda and one I hadn't seen before, although I had the feeling that I'd heard her. She had to be Frella in the flesh — although not so much of it as I had expected, judging from her voice. Not an Earth Mother type, but definitely the possessive sort. She was clinging to Teddy's arm like a starving leech. It was obvious that, in the tug-of-war to the altar, Teddy had never had a chance. I found I was beginning to feel sorry for the man — at least, I would have been if I wasn't going to have to relinquish Cho-Cho to him shortly.

Smiling and chatting, they advanced towards the buffet, pausing every few steps to allow one or another of them to acknowledge congratulations and compliments from well-wishers. Everyone was basking in the glow of success and —

Suddenly, I knew what was meant by 'thundering silence'. It had fallen upon the gathering like a striking bolt of lightning. All heads were turned to look in one direction, every breath seemed to be held. I turned, too.

Soroya. She was making an entrance from the opposite side of the stage and was on a collision course with Teddy and his group, a purposeful gleam in her eye.

241

She was looking better than I had ever seen her, wearing a sari of an exquisite shimmering iridescent material so beautiful that I had to remind myself that it would do all those expensive caps on my teeth no good at all if I ground them in envy. I settled for a wistful sigh instead.

'I've come straight from filming!' she announced in carrying tones. 'That's why I'm still in costume. But I couldn't stay away from the theatre on my dear daughter's night of triumph!'

Every drop of blood seemed to drain from Teddy's face. He shook Matilda's hand off his arm and pushed her forward into Soroya's path, while he backed away, trying to drag Frella with him. In contrast, Frella's face had gone dark red and she was glaring hatred at Soroya.

I became aware that Superintendent Thursby was watching even more avidly than the others. Was he just enjoying the drama, or was he taking a professional interest in the proceedings?

'Mmwaah! Mmwaah!' Soroya caught Matilda as she stumbled forward and planted firm kisses on both cheeks. 'I'm so proud of you! And what clever make-up — it's put so many years on you!'

'Thank you.' Matilda flinched but, conscious of her agog audience, managed a wan smile.

Teddy wasn't as expert as Eddie at the vanishing act, but Eddie hadn't been trying to drag a reluctant partner along with him. If looks could kill, Frella would have finished off Soroya then and there. Then Frella turned her head and the full blast of her murderous gaze was directed at me.

What had I ever done to her? I reeled under the force of her hatred. We hadn't even been introduced yet. Did she hold a grudge because Evangeline and I had been talking during her rehearsals? But she wasn't glaring at Evangeline.

'Do help yourself to the buffet,' Matilda said, trying to distract Soroya's attention.

'Perhaps just a bite, but I can't stay too long,' Soroya trumpeted. 'I must get back to the film crew. It's a beautiful moonlit night outside and, from certain angles, the Royal Pavilion can be made to double for the Taj Mahal.'

' "In the dark with a light behind it",' Evangeline muttered.

'Exactly!' Soroya beamed. 'All those domes and minarets. Just a bit of soft focus and night-lit long shots and it can pass for a lot of Indian locations. We do a great deal of shooting here.'

An almost inaudible sigh went up from her audience. Mine weren't the only capped teeth in danger as a wave of envy swept over the lesser lights of the production. I made a mental bet that there'd be a lot of strollers past the Royal Pavilion late tonight, all hoping to be noticed and, possibly, considered for a part in a future production. Tentative smiles were sent in Soroya's direction and a few people moved closer to her.

I had half-turned away from her, hoping that she might not notice I was holding Cho-Cho in my arms. ('What elephant?', as the comic asked innocently, trying to pretend he was unaware of the lumbering hulk following him across the stage.) It didn't work.

'I'm glad to see —' Soroya approached me and she spoke in the tone of one commending a half-witted servant for having unexpectedly done something right — 'that you're taking good care of Cho-Cho-San. I'm quite tied up for the next few days, but I'll collect her when I'm free.'

'Right.' This did not seem the moment to inform her that Teddy had reclaimed custody and I was just stealing a little time with my darling. When Soroya had time to bother, she and Teddy could fight it out between them.

She inclined her head graciously and sailed off in the direction of the buffet. A couple of hopefuls followed her, seizing their opportunity to make contact over a quail egg or vol-au-vent.

'Trixie!' Evangeline was at my side, quivering with indignation. 'It's for you!' She ground the words out from between clenched teeth, brandishing her cellphone as though she'd like to hit me with it. 'Can't you stop that woman from calling you on my mobile? Why don't you get one of your own?'

'Hello, Martha.' I took the phone uneasily, not because of Evangeline's disapproval but because, really, it was a bit late for Martha to be calling. 'Is everything all right? Hugh? The children? . . . The book?'

'Yes, yes, they're all fine. How did the show go?'

'Roaring success. It will run for ever when it hits the West End.'

'Mother . . . are you sure you're really happy about not being in it? No regrets?'

'None at all,' I said blithely. 'It will be so much better for us to star in a new show. Revivals are all very well, but . . .'

'Because,' Martha went on, 'if the show has a very long run, everyone may not stay the course. It might be necessary to replace the stars if they fall ill or get bored. I realize that Hugh isn't producing it, but he knows all the other managements and he could put in a good word —'

'Martha,' I said coldly, 'just what are you trying to tell me?'

'What is it?' Evangeline demanded. 'What's the matter?'

'I'm trying to find out,' I said grimly. 'Martha, answer me! What's wrong?'

'I went to a party tonight.' Typically, Martha took the long way round. 'One of those showbiz things Hugh has to drop in on to keep up with what's going on. Do you know, I'm quite pleased at how many people I knew there. I feel as though I'm really getting to be part of London life —'

'Martha . . .' I warned.

Cho-Cho decided her perch in my arms was now too uncomfortable with me using one hand for the phone and Evangeline crowding closer to try to hear. She dropped to the floor and stalked away.

'Yes, well, we didn't know what sort of a party it was — until it was too late.'

'Martha!' I gasped, visions of lurid headlines besetting me. 'It wasn't — You weren't —'

'No, no, nothing like that, Mother. It was all perfectly respectable and quite impromptu. I . . . er . . . saw that fellow . . . you know, the one who's supposed to be writing that new show for you . . .'

'What do you mean, "supposed to be"?'

'What?' Evangeline crowded closer. Cho-Cho would have been crushed if she hadn't decided to abandon her perch. 'What?'

'I didn't realize — not until we all got into cars and headed for Heathrow — and then it was too late — that it was a Going Away Party.'

'*Who* was going away?' But a sinking feeling in the pit of my stomach, combined with Martha's reluctance to come to the point, told me that I could make a good guess at the answer.

'Your playwright and his girlfriend. They said he'd come into some money and was taking a year off — maybe longer — to see the world. Someone mentioned six months in the South Seas, for a starter. Mother, you didn't pay him up front, did you?'

'*I* didn't,' I said meaningly and looked at Evangeline. Those cheques she had been handing out to Nigel — had Nigel been acting as a go-between to keep me from knowing she was being so foolish?

'I didn't, either!' Evangeline was now ear-to-ear with me, the mobile sandwiched

247

uncomfortably between us. Should I believe her? Of course she'd say that . . . now.

'I thought you ought to know as soon as possible, Mother. So that you can start making other plans. Or accept any offers that might come your way.'

'That's very thoughtful of you, dear,' I said.

'As if wild horses could drag Cecile off the stage after tonight!' Evangeline snorted.

Eddie had lost some of their enthusiasm on realizing that it was going to be a long time before the barley water was ready to drink — and they were unlikely to be around then.

Jocasta slumped back into her chair, her brief flurry of activity having exhausted her. She, too, seemed depressed by the knowledge that, however much she longed for it, her barley water wouldn't be ready for several long hours.

'Never mind.' I tried to lighten the sense of anticlimax that had swept over us. 'We can have some —'

The front door slammed loudly, there was a thunder of footsteps charging towards us. A man's voice bellowed:

'Where is she? Where's my little darling?'

Chapter Twelve

Jocasta shrank back in her chair, quivering. Again, I wondered about her past — and whether it had just caught up with her.

But the oldish young man — or youngish older man — who dashed into the kitchen ignored her and rushed towards Cho-Cho-San, who pranced forward to greet him with a delight she had not shown for Soroya.

'There she is!' He swept Cho-Cho-San into his arms and they nuzzled each other enthusiastically.

'If only he could get that much projection into his "Charge",' Dame Cecile sighed to Evangeline as they followed him into the room.

'Where have you been?' he asked Cho-Cho. 'I thought I'd lost you. I was so relieved when Cecile told me you were here.' His voice throbbed with emotion.

Now here was a man who would have been devastated to have had Cho-Cho returned to him as a prime example of the taxidermist's art. I studied him with interest.

poseful tread. Jocasta flinched at each step.

No, she was not in any shape to face the motorway traffic back to London today.

Equally, she wasn't in any shape to take over any housekeeping duties, either. Especially not cooking. So much for Evangeline's nefarious little scheme.

'I'm sorry.' Jocasta turned to me. 'I'm letting Martha down. I'm letting everyone down. I've never done anything like this before.'

That was obvious. 'It's all right,' I soothed. 'I've talked to Martha and she understands.'

'But she shouldn't have to understand! There shouldn't be anything to understand.' Jocasta gave a pitiful moan. 'I'll never forgive myself!' Her hand shook as she lifted the glass of water to her lips and took a sip.

'How about a cup of coffee?' I suggested. 'I'm making some for Nigel.'

'I don't want coffee!' The quick wan smile apologized for the momentary petulance. 'I want . . . I want barley water!'

'Oh?' I'd read about people drinking it in English novels, but I hadn't the faintest idea what it was. 'I'm afraid I don't —'

'Never mind,' she said despairingly. 'It's too late.'

'Too late?' I eyed her nervously. Had she taken something deadly? Was she suicidal? What did we know about her, after all? She had appeared from nowhere, with no one to vouch for her history. 'You're not — ?'

'Oh, no.' She mustered a feeble laugh. 'Nothing like that. I mean, it's just that barley water takes a long time to steep. It should have been made last night.'

'Ah — I could pop round to the local shop and pick up a bottle for you.' Nigel beamed at her magnanimously. It was not as though she had expressed a desire for Château l'Extravagance. Even he could run to a bottle of barley water.

'No. Thank you.' She dashed his hopes. 'The homemade is so much better — and so easy If only you start in time.' She glanced at me. 'I should tell Martha. It's ideal for the book. One can make it just before going out in the morning and it will be ready to drink when one comes home after the performance in the evening.'

'I'd like to make some myself.' She was perking up and anything that took her mind off her parlous state was to be encouraged. 'I could make some now. If you'd tell me how.'

'Nothing easier —' She broke off and looked around with sudden mistrust. 'If

Chapter Eighteen

'Aaaah — there she is!' Teddy reappeared suddenly alone and with the air of a man who had nearly forgotten something. 'So kind of you to look after my little fluffball for me.' With those unfeeling words, he snatched Cho-Cho-San from my arms and bore her away.

After the news from Martha, that was just about the last straw. My only comfort had been in retrieving Cho-Cho and fussing over her.

'Come along.' With unusual tact, Evangeline took one of my empty arms and steered me towards the exit. 'Time we went home. I'd say tomorrow is another day, except that we're well into tomorrow now.'

Numbly, I allowed her to lead me away. Eddie was waiting outside with the taxi. I would have asked him where he'd been, but I couldn't trust my voice. I blinked against the moisture obscuring my vision. I didn't want Eddie. I didn't want Evangeline. I wanted Cho-Cho to come home with me. I slumped into a corner of the back seat and ignored their efforts to cheer me.

Morning was no better.

'Pull yourself together!' Evangeline snapped the most useless words in the world at me.

'Shan't!' I brooded into a bowl of soggy cornflakes, topped with mushy slices of a banana long past its 'best by' date. The sooner this establishment found a decent housekeeper, the better.

'Do you realize that this was my first opening in nearly twenty years when I didn't have my little Fleur cheering me on?' Dame Cecile, the thrill of last night's ovations fading into memory, was doing some brooding of her own. 'I don't know how I managed to go on.'

'You were magnificent, Cecile.' Evangeline was prepared to be more forbearing with her old friend than with me. 'And you, too, Matilda,' she added hastily.

'It *did* go rather well.' Matilda managed to sound modest while still glowing with triumph. There was nothing on her horizon to dim her achievement.

'Is this all we're having for breakfast?' That is, not until Soroya stalked into the there's any barley in the house.'

'Don't worry,' I assured her. 'We went shopping yesterday while you were . . . er . . . out of it. We're all stocked up.' With chicken soup in mind, I had bought barley, rice and all kinds of pasta for the store cupboard. Even several tins of new potatoes and, with Cho-Cho in mind, tins of tuna, salmon and mackerel fillets. We were loaded for bear.

'Lemons?' She was still wary. 'Fresh lemons? Unwaxed?'

'Lemons, limes, oranges,' I answered proudly. 'Also —'

'Just lemons. You can also make it with oranges or limes, but lemons are best — so far as I'm concerned. Now . . .' She was almost back to normal. 'A quart jug. Is there a quart jug around?'

'If there is, I'll find it.' Entering into the spirit of the occasion, Eddie began opening cabinet doors. 'This right?' He held up his find.

'Good. Get the kettle boiling —' She flung out the order and they both jumped to obey.

'Tea strainer . . .' That was to hand. She scooped two heaped tablespoons of barley pearls into it and rinsed them thoroughly under the cold water tap and emptied the strainer into the jug.

'And a grater for the lemon . . .' I'd noticed something of the sort in a cutlery drawer earlier. I found it again and brought it to her.

'We just want the zest.' She had swung into teaching mode. 'That is, the yellow part,' she translated for the men. 'None of the pith — the white stuff — or the juice.' Expertly, she denuded the lemon of its colour, grating it into the jug.

'And now, some sugar . . .'

Her willing accolytes leaped for the sugar bowl and Nigel won. He proffered it to her. She ladled a couple of spoonfuls into the jug.

'If that's not enough, you can add more when you come to drink it. Now, kettle boiling? Good.' She filled the jug with the boiling water and stepped back.

We waited expectantly for the next step. She looked back at us and shrugged.

'That's it,' she said. 'Perhaps a saucer over the top . . .' She suited action to words. 'And that's really all there is to it. Just let it stand until it cools, then pop it into the fridge to steep overnight, or while you're out all day Then strain it and drink it. Nothing could be easier.'

'Wonderful!' I exclaimed.

'Ah . . . !' 'Yeah . . .' Both Nigel and

room and glowered at the box of corn-flakes. 'No devilled kidneys? No kedgeree? I've worked until dawn. I need something better than this to keep my strength up!'

As one, we turned to regard her coldly. The temperature in the room instantly dropped at least ten degrees.

'This is insufferable!' Soroya was back to normal. All that joy and delight in her 'daughter's' success she had been babbling about last night had evaporated without an audience she could impress. 'Have you contacted the agency yet? We must get a housekeeper!'

'I *have* been rather busy with other concerns,' Matilda retorted icily.

'Oh, yes, you're your father's daughter, all right,' Soroya said, as though there might have been any doubt about it. 'You're all the same — your generation —'

Matilda stiffened. Her head reared back and her eyes flashed fire.

'Selfish and thoughtless!' Heedless of the danger signals, Soroya began listing the genetic shortcomings. 'Always putting yourself first. Never a thought for anyone else —'

'That will be quite enough!' Matilda stood up abruptly. 'I will not be insulted in my own home in front of my own guests.'

'Your father's home,' Soroya corrected.

251

'If it weren't for him, you wouldn't be here.'

The same could be said of Soroya. Matilda took a deep breath and seemed about to say it, then recollected her guests. She glared at Soroya instead.

'I don't expect gratitude, which is just as well.' Soroya wrapped a martyr's cloak around her. 'I allow you to occupy the house rent-free in my absence. I never complain about your filling it with your friends and hangers-on —'

'Just try charging rent!' Matilda flared. 'This is my house! My father never contributed a penny — not to the house, nor to my support, nor my mother's. He preferred to throw his money away on . . . on his latest doxy!'

'Not another word!' Soroya drew herself up imperiously. 'I will not listen to you sully your father's memory. Nor will I be foolish enough to expect any sort of apology from you — now or in the future. We will not speak of this matter again!' She turned on her heel and sailed out of the room.

'Of all the women my father toyed with,' Matilda finally broke the silence, 'that had to be the one he married!'

'More to the point,' Evangeline said, 'she

was the one he was married to when he died. She wouldn't have lasted much longer than the others, if he'd remained alive and true to form.'

It was a nice try at comfort, but could have been more tactful. After all, Matilda's mother was high on the roster of ex-wives.

'I've got to do something about this!' Matilda slumped back into her chair despairingly, burying her face in her hands. 'Now that they're doing more filming in this country, she's planning to take up residence. I can stand her for short periods of time, but not indefinitely. I've got to do something!'

'Frame a copy of your deeds and hang them on the wall in her room,' Dame Cecile suggested. 'Make sure it's just a copy.'

'Throw her out.' Evangeline was all for simplicity. 'Just change the locks while she's away filming and leave her packed suitcases outside the front door.'

'And wouldn't that give the tabloids a field day?' Matilda was more practical. 'I don't need that kind of publicity.'

'Quite right,' Dame Cecile said. 'It would do the show no good, either. It may be a hit, but we can't afford to be complacent.'

There was a clatter at the back door and it swung open. Eddie stumbled into the kitchen, laden down with toolbox, cans of paint and brushes.

'I'll 'ave those bookcases finished for you before lunch,' he told Matilda. 'Then I'll paint them. Tomorrow —' he turned to me — 'I'll take care of that dodgy shelf in your closet.'

'Wonderful!' Matilda enthused. 'I don't know what we'd do without you, Eddie.'

'Yeah, right, that's all very well and I don't mean to be nasty — but I wish you *were* doing without me. I mean, 'ow much longer can they make me stay 'ere? I've got a life — and it's up in London. I want to get back to it.'

'You should have asked Superintendent Thursby about that last night,' I said. 'He was at the opening and you saw him — and you went the other way.'

'Yeah, well, I remembered something else I 'ad to do.' He avoided my eyes. 'Anyway, you don't always want to remind the coppers that you're still around.'

'If they don't remember you're around,' I pointed out reasonably, 'they can't tell you you're free to go.'

'Right. I just don't like the bloke. I'll tell you this, there's some difference in the coppers now and when you're driving a cab full of deprived kiddies down to the seaside on their annual outing, which is the only time I saw the coppers here before.'

'Yes, but you're on the other side of the law now,' Evangeline said pleasantly.

'Yeah . . .' He slitted his eyes at her. 'And I know who I've got to thank for that, don't I?'

'Circumstances, circumstances . . .' Evangeline waved her hand airily. 'These things could happen to anyone.'

'But they don't. They only 'appen to you.' He gave her a bleak look. 'And to me, when I'm around you.'

'Yes,' Evangeline said, 'I'm afraid we have been a bit remiss about you. Don't worry.' He immediately looked worried. 'We'll talk to Superintendent Thursby and get you sorted out.'

'Look,' he said, 'you don't need to go near the police. What about that lawyer who got me out on bail? Let 'im do it.'

'Nonsense! It's Thursby's case. He'll know just what's going on. We'll take him to lunch, or perhaps dinner, and have a long, friendly discuss—' Her mobile trilled abruptly.

'Oh, for heaven's sake!' She snatched it from her bag and flung it at me. 'Tell that woman to use the land line and stop ringing my number! I don't keep the phone for her convenience — or yours, either!'

'Sorry,' I said, catching it. 'She doesn't mean to —' I broke off. Apologies were premature. It was Nigel's voice bleating at me.

'Evangeline? Evangeline? Who's there? I want to speak to Evangeline.'

'It's for you.' I handed the mobile back to her and watched her face change as she listened to Nigel's frantic tones.

'What do you mean?' Her voice was as thunderous as her face. 'You told me I couldn't lose!'

I couldn't hear the words but the frantic pitch of the babbled explanations and reassurances was unmistakable. There went another of Nigel's get-rich-quick schemes down the drain — and this time it was carrying Evangeline along with it.

'You promised!' The incredulity in her voice belied the fact that both of us had learned a long time ago never to trust a promise, any promise, no matter who made it.

The high-pitched babble rushed on nonstop. Evangeline's face relaxed as she gradually allowed herself to be mollified. Obviously with more promises.

'See that you do!' she said severely and rang off. 'That's settled,' she told me. 'Now — let's tackle dear Superintendent Thursby.'

Somewhere between the lobster bisque and the steak au poivre, I began to suspect that Superintendent Hector Thursby was toying with us. By the Poires Hélène, I was sure of it. By the time the demitasses, petits fours and mints arrived, I was convinced that it was his sole ambition to make complete and utter fools of us.

He was going about it the right way, concentrating on Evangeline, leading her on to ever more outrageous statements and speculations. She had just stated as fact her opinion that Mr Stuff Yours had been involved with international jewel thieves, who were stuffing precious gems into the body cavities of dead animals and smuggling them into the country that way. And out of the country as well.

'Mmm, yes,' he murmured. 'I seem to think I saw that television play, too.'

'And what about drugs?' Evangeline was not to be daunted. 'That would be a perfect way to smuggle drugs into the country. Have you had the ashes tested for traces of drugs?'

'There are rather a lot of ashes.' His murmur remained diffident, but a telltale twitch at the corners of his mouth gave him away. 'Have you any suggestions as to where we might start?'

I tried to signal caution, but she was paying no attention.

'How about that horse? It was big enough to hold half a warehouse worth of drugs.'

'Yes, it was big, wasn't it? However, it dates back to 1937, favourite hunter of a local lord, had to be shot when it broke its neck in a nasty fall. He had it mounted and kept it in his conservatory. Upon his death in 1981, the family donated it to a small private museum — with great relief, no doubt. It's been there ever since, until about six months ago when it went to Stuff Yours for some minor repairs and a brush-up. It was scheduled to go straight back into the museum when finished.'

'Oh.' That took the wind out of Evangeline's sails, but only momentarily. 'Then how about — ?'

'Amazingly well documented, wasn't it?' I put in. What was really amazing was that Thursby should have had all that information at his fingertips. He'd been doing more homework than Evangeline was giving him credit for.

'Bit of a local curiosity, that horse.' He shrugged off his expertise. 'Newspapers run articles about it when not much else is happening. And, once in a while, organizations borrow it for parades or promotions.'

'Smuggling, jewellery thefts, drugs —' Abruptly, Evangeline swept them all aside with a wave of her hand. 'The point is, Eddie can't possibly have had anything to do with any of that. It's high time you allowed him to go back to London.'

'Oh, I don't know.' Thursby bared his teeth ('What *very* big teeth you have, Grandmother') in a grim smile. 'Some people might think a taxi driver ideally placed to act as a fence or drug dealer. Driving all over the city, with no suspicion attached to any place he stops. It would go down well with the shady customers too. They could call him and he'd meet them anywhere.'

'Never!' I said. 'Not Eddie!' If that was the way he was thinking, no wonder he wouldn't let Eddie leave town.

'Complete nonscnsc!' Evangeline said. 'No wonder you aren't getting anywhere with the case if you're wasting your time trying to trump up evidence against an innocent man!'

Oh-oh! She'd gone too far. The planes of his face shifted subtly and hardened. A nasty gleam came into his eyes.

'She didn't mean —' I began defensively.

'I think she made her meaning quite clear,' he said.

A cold chill swept over me. Abruptly, I remembered Ron Heyhoe's story about the rugby match and the almost-permanent injury Thursby had deliberately inflicted on him. We'd laughed when he gave us our introduction because he said he owed Thursby one. Now — too late? — I recalled uneasily that there had been times when Heyhoe had had his problems with Evangeline. Did he feel that he owed us one, too?

'Just what makes you think we aren't getting anywhere with the case?' His glittering eyes were as cold and menacing as those of the hooded cobra must have been, and Evangeline was momentarily as frozen in their beam as any lesser prey.

'You haven't told us anything! What else are we to think?' No, Evangeline was more mongoose than prey; she came out fighting.

'You might think that it was none of your business. You might think that it was just possible that the police had more than one case at a time to work on. You might even think that your own position was a bit equivocal. You were on the scene, you have a highly developed sense of drama and, I understand, a fearsome temperament. If you had quarrelled with the man, struck him impulsively, harder than you meant to . . . ?' He gave a cold smile and paused, inviting a confession.

'Don't be ridiculous!'

'It's only too plausible, I assure you. As is the possibility that your friend Eddie is so good a friend that he is allowing himself to be chief suspect in order to shield you.'

'No!' I gasped with outrage and he transferred his icy gaze to me.

'Both of you,' he said impartially.

'Really!' Evangeline's head reared back, her nostrils flared. 'You'll be accusing Cecile next!'

'We're not dismissing her out of hand. My information is that she is an extremely distraught woman whose recent behaviour has been . . . eccentric . . . if not demented.'

'Who gave you that information?'

'Now, now.' He shook his head. 'You should know that we never reveal our sources.'

'Not unless it suits you!'

I noticed the waiter hovering as our dis-

261

cussion grew more heated and signalled to him urgently. It took him only a moment to deliver the bill which, after hesitating briefly, he set down beside the gentleman of the party.

I could see that Evangeline was so furious she was going to let it stay there, so I grabbed it.

'We *did* invite him,' I whispered.

'And very kind of you, too.' He wasn't missing a thing. 'A delicious meal and a most enjoyable occasion.'

I was glad he thought so.

Chapter Nineteen

In the morning, I didn't feel like facing
Eddie, even though I knew he had never expected our efforts with Superintendent
Thursby to be successful. Cravenly, I decided to skip breakfast at the house and go
out and buy that pretty necklace for Viola,
getting something to eat at a coffee shop
along the way. Let Evangeline be the one to
break the bad news to Eddie when he arrived, it had been her idea. Not one of her
better ones. We were now firmly placed in
the forefront of Thursby's attention. And
suspicion.

It was a good plan: I might have known
it wouldn't work. When I got back to the
house, Evangeline was still in bed. That
took care of the glow of triumph I felt over
my successful purchases. I'd picked up a
novelty watch for Orlando, so that he
wouldn't feel neglected, and a couple of
kitchen gadgets for Martha.

'One of her headaches,' Dame Cecile informed me. 'And that terrible smell of
paint isn't going to help.'

Now that she mentioned it, I became aware of the overpowering odour of fresh paint. Eddie was putting the finishing touches to Matilda's new built-in bookcase. Perhaps he'd have time to fix my closet shelf while the first coat of paint was drying.

I decided to clear the clothes rail suspended from that shelf, so that Eddie could get at it more easily. There wasn't much hanging from it and, as I worked, I allowed myself the brief luxury of imagining that I could throw everything back into my suitcase, ready to depart.

But we couldn't leave yet. We couldn't desert Eddie. And perhaps the 'don't leave town' edict had been extended to us by this time. Hector Thursby seemed to be preparing an all-purpose, any-suspect-will-do case against one or all of us.

The unused wire hangers at the far end of the rail were in a fearful tangle. They had been rammed over the rail carelessly, their hooks opening in opposite directions, their loops intertwined and practically tied in knots. They had probably been there so long they were all rusted together. I tugged impatiently at them.

Suddenly, the whole thing gave way. I had time for one sharp involuntary scream as the shelf tilted and an avalanche plunged towards me.

'. . . Trixie! . . . Trixie! . . .' People were calling to me from a great distance, their voices faint and alarmed. 'Trixie! . . .'

I moaned and turned over. I didn't want to wake up. I wanted to lie here on this nice comfortable bed for ever.

'Trixie!'

I tried to pull the pillow over my ears, but a sudden pain shot through my head and jolted my eyes open. I moaned again.

'She's coming round.'

'I'm not. Go away and —' Someone pulled me upright and thrust a glass of water against my lips. I discovered I was very thirsty.

'Trixie — what happened?'

'The shelf got me,' I said. 'Before Eddie had a chance to fix it.'

'I was going to get at it right after lunch,' he defended himself. 'Couldn't you leave well enough alone until then?'

'I just wanted to clear the rail for you, but the hangers were all stuck together and, when I pulled at them, the whole shelf —'

'Eddie's right,' Evangeline said. 'If you didn't go rushing at things —'

'The edge of the shelf didn't strike you,

did it?' Matilda looked me over carefully. 'I don't see any blood.'

'She might have concussion.' Dame Cecile was as ready as Evangeline with ever the encouraging word. 'How many fingers am I holding up?'

'I'm not going to answer that.' My head was settling down to a steady throbbing ache. 'Why doesn't somebody get me some aspirin?'

'They might not be the best thing for you,' Matilda worried. 'I'll call the doctor. That shelf could have done serious damage.'

'I don't need a doctor —'

'It wasn't the shelf.' Eddie had roamed over to inspect the closet. 'That's still 'anging in there. Only just, mind you, but . . .' Eddie moved deeper into the closet, then we heard a clatter, as though he had stepped into a nest of wire hangers, and a muffled oath.

'Are you all right?' Matilda called.

'Just about.' He reappeared in the doorway, a cluster of coat hangers in one hand, a largish suitcase in the other. 'It's dangerous in there.'

'So Trixie discovered,' Evangeline said.

'They say most accidents happen in the home,' Dame Cecile said, 'and this home is well on the way to proving it.'

'I'm going to need room to work in there.' Eddie turned to me. 'Where do you want me to put your suitcase?'

'That isn't mine,' I said. 'Mine's over there.'

He turned to Matilda.

'It's certainly not mine,' Matilda said. 'I've never seen it before in my life.'

'Oh . . . ?' He stood there, holding the old-fashioned, slightly battered case, then revolved it slowly, inspecting it.

'Stop!' Evangeline shouted. 'Hold it right there!'

He did and suddenly we all saw it: a Qantas Airways label stuck on one end of the case.

'Where did you say that housekeeper was from?' Evangeline asked.

'Australia,' Matilda said faintly, staring at the label. 'You think it was hers?'

'We can open it and find out. Set it down on the chair, Eddie, and let's take a look at it.' Evangeline moved forward purposefully. 'I don't suppose you saw any sign of a key?'

'Probably 'ave to bust it open.' Eddie poked at the lock.

'We can't do that,' Matilda protested.

'Why not?' Eddie wanted to know.

'Who's going to complain?'

'He's right.' Evangeline was stabbing at the lock with a nail file. 'Until we look inside, we won't know who has any right to complain — not that they would. If we hadn't opened it they'd never have known what happened to her.'

'I'll get my toolkit.' Eddie hurried off. 'You'll never do it that way.'

'I suppose we must.' Matilda surrendered. 'The police were asking about her next-of-kin and I wasn't able to tell them. I'd like to know myself. I should write to them, see what arrangements . . .'

'*If* there's any information inside.' I tried to sound a warning before they got too hopeful about it.

'There's bound to be some clue.' Evangeline would not be discouraged. 'Eddie —' He was back. 'Have a go!'

'Right!' He attacked the lock with a hammer and chisel.

I sank back on the bed and this time succeeded in folding the pillow around my ears, not that it did much good in blocking out the noise. Vaguely, it occurred to me that, if the shelf was still in place, it must have been the suitcase that hit me, sliding off the shelf when it tilted. That meant someone had pushed it as far back on the shelf as it could go. Trying to hide it? Or just tidying it out of sight, as a good house-keeper would have done?

The hammering stopped abruptly. I heard Evangeline's satisfied exclamation and sat up again, struggling off the bed and over to join the others around the case.

'There!' Eddie wrenched back the lid and we looked down at the neat piles of clothing.

There were the usual bulging pockets along all sides of the case, the most logical places to look for any papers. Still, something held us back. I was sure I was not the only one to have a lump in my throat. She hadn't even had time to unpack.

'It's got to be done!' Evangeline's rallying call seemed to be for herself as much as for us. She plunged her hands into the most bulging of the pockets.

We looked with sad dismay at the dubious trophies she pulled out: a half-used jar of foundation cream, a couple of lipsticks, an eyebrow pencil, an eyeliner — cosmetics for a face that would never need them again.

Shaken, Evangeline dropped the pathetic hoard on top of a folded blouse and slid her hand into another side pocket with less enthusiasm. This time, she felt cautiously along the pocket making sure that what she found might have some relevance to our quest. The heavy-duty manilla envelope she surfaced with looked distinctly more promising.

It wasn't sealed, it just had one of those little metal clasps. Evangeline bent the wings back and slid the flap open. The contents seemed promisingly bulky. Surely there must be something in there.

'Why don't we take it downstairs — ?' Matilda began, but Evangeline was already pulling out the papers.

A few letters in yellowing envelopes looked a likely source of information, but would take time to read. Evangeline was after more immediate results. She let the letters slide back into the big envelope and flipped through the remaining documents until — paydirt!

'A passport!' Evangeline said. 'Now we're getting somewhere!'

She opened it eagerly. A strange expression came over her face as she read it. Wordlessly, she handed it to Matilda.

'Alison Temple-Jordan,' Matilda read out. 'But what —'

'Wait . . .' Evangeline had found an official-looking document. 'Here's a birth certificate.' She read it before holding it out to

Matilda, who took it gingerly.

'Mother . . . Margaret Temple. Father . . .' Matilda's voice trembled. 'Gervaise Jordan.'

'The old bastard!' Evangeline said. 'Sorry, Matilda, but —'

Matilda hadn't heard her. She stood frozen in time and space. I crowded forward to look at the documents and my heart twisted with pity for the poor woman who had reached out for that spurious hyphen to give her baby the illusion of legitimacy, so desperately important in those days.

'She . . . she was my half-sister,' Matilda whispered, 'and . . . I never knew.'

'She wanted you to get to know her before she told you.' Dame Cecile patted her shoulder comfortingly, but she was oblivious.

'I liked her . . . I liked her the minute I saw her. That was why I hired her. I thought we could be friends —' Matilda's voice broke.

'Downstairs!' Evangeline ordered briskly. 'Downstairs — and drinks all round. We need them!'

'At least we now know who her next-of-kin is.' Matilda's mouth twisted wryly. 'I am.'

Chapter Twenty

'Of course she'll go on tonight,' Evangeline re-assured Dame Cecile. 'Best thing for her. Keep to the routine, keep her mind off . . . things.'

'But you'll come along?' Dame Cecile had a death grip on Evangeline's arm. 'You know the part — at least, you can fake it.'

'Faking won't be necessary,' Evangeline said coldly, while I contemplated the understudy's probable reaction to that turn of events. She wouldn't like it. A complaint to Equity might even ensue.

'Evangeline,' I said cautiously, 'I'm not sure —'

'Both of you!' Now I found my own arm caught in that iron grip. 'She's stunned, horrified, in a state of shock. Anything could happen.'

'We'll be there,' Evangeline promised. 'But not because we're worried about Matilda. You got Teddy up to the mark for the opening. I'm concerned to see that he stays there.'

First night nerves over and success assured, the cast were clearly enjoying themselves almost as much as the audience. Teddy seemed to have learned his lesson, delivering his lines robustly, although with an occasional nervous sidelong glance at Cecile. Matilda worked smoothly, giving no hint of her private troubles.

Even better, Frella didn't hate me any more. She smiled pleasantly when introduced and gave no sign of ever having seen me before — offstage, that is.

If I hadn't been so shaken by her earlier hostility, I might have convinced myself I had imagined it. Especially when she included me in the invitation to return home with her and the others for an after-the-show supper.

She and Teddy had rented a pleasant, nondescriptly furnished flat within walking distance of the theatre. I looked around it with more than passing interest. The decor didn't bother me, I was looking for Cho-Cho.

'Nothing elaborate, I'm afraid,' Frella said briskly — and how right she was. She decanted a couple of cartons of the kind of commercial soup that claims it's home-made into a large saucepan and, opening the fridge, pulled out two containers of store-bought sandwiches packaged in rows of neat triangles.

'Not much time for domesticity lately.' Teddy herded us into the living room before we could discover any more culinary short cuts and began opening the wine.

At the sound of his voice, a small head poked around the corner and surveyed the room cautiously. Unusually, she hadn't rushed into the kitchen immediately upon hearing the snick of the fridge door opening and closing. Perhaps she had been asleep.

'There's my little darling!' Teddy boomed, catching sight of her.

Now she advanced into the room with increasing boldness, sure of her welcome. I snapped my fingers at her and cooed but, for some reason, she chose to 'go over to Cecile, who hadn't even noticed her.

'Won't be long . . .' Frella called from the kitchen over the rattle of crockery.

'No hurry,' Teddy called back. 'We're quite comfortable. I'll bring you your drink.' He poured ours and carried Frella's into the kitchen.

'Oh!' Dame Cecile gave a muffled exclamation. Cho-Cho had suddenly crouched and leaped into her lap. She started to push her away but, as her fingers touched the soft fur, the push turned into a tentative stroke, then another. Cecile was missing Fleur so much that any fur was comforting. Cho-Cho settled down in her lap and I tried to control a certain amount of jealousy. Why hadn't Cho-Cho come to me?

'Soup's on its way.' Teddy carried in a large chipped-edge platter on to which the sandwich triangles had been transferred and garnished with tiny gherkins, cherry tomatoes and some indefinable greenish bits which might have been mustard cress, parsley, or possibly beansprouts. I did not intend to find out.

Matilda had gone very quiet; the adrenaline rush which had carried her through the performance had dissipated and sent her into a low. I wondered if she had realized yet that she was going to have to talk to the police in the morning and tell them what we had discovered. Even though it might start Superintendent Thursby wondering if they ought to look more closely into the housekeeper's death, now that her identity made her someone Matilda might have a motive for disposing of. Thursby was uncomfortably eager to suspect everyone — hitherto Matilda had been the only one he hadn't considered.

For a moment, I allowed myself to explore the possibility. If the housekeeper had moved in and couldn't wait to reveal herself to Matilda, might Matilda have reacted murderously? Already beset by a stepmother she couldn't stand and now faced with an unexpected half-sibling — another unwanted legacy from her problem parent, another millstone around her neck — it would not be completely surprising if something had snapped.

Matilda looked over at me and smiled wanly just then and I felt as guilty as though she could read my mind. But no — the trap had already been set and waiting. Perhaps for Matilda herself? No, I exonerated her to my own satisfaction. Besides, if she were going to start killing her encumbrances, she would have finished off Soroya years ago. But I was afraid Superintendent Thursby wouldn't be so easily convinced.

'Teddy, could you please — ?' Frella appeared in the doorway and abruptly froze. An almost palpable wave of hatred emanated from her and swept across the room. I was stunned.

This time, she hated Cecile. Was the woman some kind of schizoid?

'The soup is ready.' Frella lowered her eyelids and turned away, but the shock wave still reverberated through the room.

'Right.' Teddy hadn't noticed, neither had anyone else. He followed her into the kitchen and returned carrying a heavy tray of mugs which he dealt out to us.

Cho-Cho lifted her head to sniff as Dame Cecile took her mug of soup from the tray, but immediately lost interest. Carrot and coriander didn't do anything for her.

I wasn't sure it did much for me, but I smiled at Teddy as I accepted my own mug.

Evangeline shifted uneasily and looked around the room; the vibes were reaching her, but she couldn't determine their source. She looked at me and raised an inquiring eyebrow. I nodded confirmation, but was not in a position to explain.

Having distributed all the mugs, Teddy now began passing the platter of sandwiches. Cho-Cho abruptly deserted Dame Cecile and went to the man with the food, twining around his ankles.

'No, no, dear heart, you'll trip me,' Teddy said fondly, managing to scratch her under the chin with the toe of his shoe without quite overbalancing. It was close, though, the sandwiches nearly landed in Matilda's lap and a cherry tomato rolled off on to the carpet.

'I'll take that!' The blast of hatred deto-
nated again — this time, Teddy was the
target. 'Before you drop it!' Frella snatched
the platter from Teddy's unresisting hands
which, happily freed, stretched down to
pick up Cho-Cho. She snuggled into his
arms, accepting his caresses, although I
noticed she kept one eye on the sandwiches.

'Pay no attention to Teddy.' Frella offered Dame Cecile the sandwiches with a
practised smile and no sign of hostility. She
hated Teddy now. 'He thinks more of that
cat than he does of me.'

Hardly surprising, the cat had a much
nicer personality. It couldn't be easy to be
married to a woman whose emotions were
about as stable as an erupting volcano.
Now she hates you, now she doesn't —
and you can never be sure when. How had
she ever managed to direct a hit play? The
woman wasn't rational.

'Than any of us,' Frella amended
smoothly, as Evangeline selected a couple
of triangles.

'Trixie?' I was aware of little eyes
watching as I made my selection. I took
the prawn mayonnaise — and that settled
it. Cho-Cho twisted from Teddy's arms,
leaped to the floor and trotted over to me.

Teddy beamed forgivingly as he saw me slide a fat juicy prawn out of the sandwich to welcome her.

Not so Frella. She drew in her breath with a hiss and I felt the full torrent of her hatred wash over me. Startled, I looked up at her. That Jekyll-and-Hyde transformation had happened again. She was back to hating me.

How could Teddy live with it day after day? And yet, Soroya had been his initial choice — he sure could pick them. Or had they picked him? Perhaps only a doormat type like Teddy could survive in symbiosis with such overpowering personalities.

Cho-Cho felt it, too. She gave Frella a wide berth as she skirted around her legs to reach me. Frella's face was a cold mask, but she could not hide the expression in her eyes as she looked at Cho-Cho. She was jealous as a cat — of a cat. She would willingly — happily — do it harm. Teddy had better not turn his back or Cho-Cho would be in danger.

But he had turned his back once before. And Cho-Cho had barely escaped a hideous fate. If we hadn't come along —

'*You* did it!' I gasped, rising to my feet to confront Frella. 'It was *you!*'

'I believe you're right,' Evangeline said, glaring at Frella.

'Did what?' Teddy stared at us, blinking, unsure of what had happened to turn a polite and friendly gathering into an armed camp.

'Don't tell him!' Frella rasped. It was half-plea, half-command. But, unlike some, I wasn't hers to command.

'What on earth . . . ?' Matilda was as nonplussed as Teddy. Cecile watched quietly, nodding understanding.

'Tell me what?' Teddy was coming to grips with the situation. He looked at Frella suspiciously. 'What don't you want me to know?'

'Nothing!' Frella would not meet his eyes.

Her prawn finished and recognizing that nothing else was likely to be immediately forthcoming, Cho-Cho strolled back to Teddy and nudged his ankle. Automatically, he stooped to pick her up.

'You and that damned cat!' Frella exploded.

'I thought you liked her.' Even Teddy couldn't miss the animosity. It bewildered him.

'Think again!' Evangeline was right there with me. 'She tried to kill her.'

Frella made a choking sound.

'What?' Teddy clutched Cho-Cho to him

280

protectively. 'What are you saying?'

'She took that cat to Stuff Yours! It was going to be returned to you stuffed and mounted.' Evangeline paused and, for good measure, added, 'And for some reason, she then murdered Mr Stuff Yours.'

'I didn't!' Frella cried. 'I never touched him. He was all right when I left him!'

Evangeline and I exchanged glances. How often had one or the other of us found that line in our scripts? At her hammiest, Evangeline had delivered it with more conviction than Frella.

'Left him? Then you *were* there . . .' Teddy was slow, but he was putting two and two together. 'You admit it! You were going to —' He clutched Cho-Cho so tightly she emitted a protesting squeak.

'And then she set the place on fire!' Dame Cecile supplied.

'I did not!' Frella's voice rose. She took a tentative step towards Teddy. 'Teddy, I swear —'

Teddy backed away. Cho-Cho flattened her ears and spat at Frella. I don't know where an innocent young cat learned language like that.

'You —' Teddy took another step backwards. 'You tried to kill Cho-Cho-San!'

'You care more for that cat than you do for me!' The bitter accusation was hurled at him with force and venom — just before Frella burst into tears.

'Frella, don't —' He broke off, visibly trying to harden his heart.

'Why not? What do you care? You've got your damned cat!'

'I thought you liked Cho-Cho. You never said anything —'

'I kept hoping Soroya would get her and take her out of the country and keep her out!'

'But she never did. And so you took my little Cho-Cho to a —' Horror filled his voice, his eyes. 'To a taxidermist!'

'That's right! Without her, I had a chance of getting some of your attention! But I didn't kill anyone — I swear to you, Teddy. And I didn't set any fires either!'

This time her declaration rang true. She might be a monster, sick with jealousy to the point of destroying an innocent cat, but she drew the line at killing a human being. And she hadn't committed arson, either.

'So what are you going to do about it?' Frella faced Teddy defiantly.

'I . . . I don't know. I can never trust you again.'

'Not with that cat, no. It's crunch time, Teddy. You have to choose between us. Which is it going to be? Her? Or me?'

Cho-Cho mewled plaintively as his arms tightened. He looked down at her, then looked at Frella. More expression than he had ever used on stage flickered across his face. He loved that cat dearly but, sweet and willing though Cho-Cho might be, she couldn't support him financially in his declining years — which were fast approaching — while Frella was firmly on track for growing success in the theatre and lots of lucrative jobs.

To be fair, perhaps he loved Frella, too — difficult though that might be to imagine. He kept looking from one to the other, his eyes filled with tears.

'I won't give her to Soroya,' he said weakly.

'You don't have to.' I put in my bid quickly. 'She's a little darling — anyone would be glad to have her.'

'To let her go away . . . never to see her again . . .' His voice shook. Frella waited.

'You can have visiting privileges,' I bargained recklessly. 'Drop in any time.' I moved forward eagerly.

'Well . . .' He was giving Cho-Cho a few final loving parting strokes. She purred unheedingly.

'That's settled then!' Dame Cecile reached him before I did and swept Cho-Cho into her arms. 'You must feel absolutely free to come and visit her any time you like.'

'Now, just a min—' Evangeline's hand closed on my arm, pulling me back.

'The revelation came to me when I held her on my lap a few minutes ago.' Dame Cecile faced us raptly. 'I remembered the story of Sir Henry Irving and his faithful dog. Like Fleur, the dog always sat in its favourite chair in his dressing room, watching him make up for the performance, greeting him when he came offstage. When the dog died, Sir Henry was distraught and heartbroken. When next he went to his dressing room in the Lyceum, it was with a sad and aching heart, dreading to face that empty chair.

'But it wasn't empty. The theatre cat, who had never gone near the dressing room while the dog was alive, strolled in and leaped up on the empty cushion, taking over the dog's guardian angelship. Sir Henry promptly sent his dresser out for fish for the cat and it became his pampered pet, watching over him as the dog had done. And when Sir Henry retired from the stage, he took the cat home with him.

'And I know, I just *know* —' Dame Cecile looked around at our stunned faces, defying any of us to gainsay her — 'that my dear little Fleur, wherever she may be, has arranged for this cat to come to me in her place and solace me in my grief!'

'But —' I tried again. Evangeline's grasp tightened.

'We're all tired,' Evangeline said smoothly. 'I think it's time we were all on our way.'

'I'll see you to the door.' Frella moved forward eagerly to speed the parting guests, ready for the big reconciliation scene as soon as we were out of the way. Teddy looked ready to collapse.

Chapter Twenty-One

I could only consider it poetic justice. As Matilda turned the key in the lock and swung the front door open, Soroya swooped on us.

'There you are at last!' she accused. 'I've been waiting up for you!'

'That makes a change,' Matilda said wearily. She walked past Soroya and up the stairs. 'Then you can lock up for the night, too.'

'And you!' Soroya whirled on Cecile. 'What are you doing with my cat? I've been looking for her everywhere!' She snatched Cho-Cho from Cecile and followed Matilda up the stairs.

'But that's my —' It was Dame Cecile's turn for a futile protest. She started after Soroya indignantly, but Evangeline stopped her.

'She's got a good case for ownership,' Evangeline warned. 'Let it be for tonight.'

'I shall complain to Teddy in the morning!'

'You do that,' I said. I locked the door myself and turned out the lights. They took the hint and let me lead them up the stairs.

The only good thing about it, I consoled myself, was that at least Cho-Cho was under the same roof with me. Furthermore, she had escaped from Soroya before — and she knew where my room was. I went to bed feeling rather more cheerful than I had been earlier in the evening.

I couldn't believe it when I got up in the morning. Evangeline was already up and had gone out. Where? And why?

'An errand of some importance, I believe.' Dame Cecile was seated at the kitchen table with a cup of coffee and some toast. 'It must be — to get her out of the house at this hour!'

'Right.' I poured my own coffee and slumped into a chair. I'd think about something to eat with the second cup. 'I don't suppose you have any idea when she might be back?' I feared the worst: if Nigel was involved, it was going to be the worst possible start to the day.

'She didn't say —' Something in the doorway caught Cecile's attention and I turned to see what it was.

'Cho-Cho!' I cried joyously. 'You got away!'

'She knows where she belongs,' Dame

Cecile said complacently. 'Here, Cho-Cho! Over here!'

Cho-Cho stopped and looked around.

'She needs a bit of training.' Dame Cecile stood and went over to her. 'One must be firm. Kind, but firm. Come, Cho-Cho, heel!'

'I don't think it works like that with cats, Cecile.' She was the one who needed training. I made affectionate noises. 'Come over here, Cho-Cho. Come to Trixie.'

'Heel, Cho-Cho!' Dame Cecile ordered, striding back to the table. 'Heel!'

Cho-Cho gave her a contemptuous look, sent me a friendly one, and made her choice. She marched straight to the fridge and pawed at the door.

'Give her some fish!' Dame Cecile ordered, obviously with the example of Sir Henry Irving in mind.

'We don't have any.'

'What do we have?'

Cho-Cho gave an impatient meow, the matter was obviously one of some urgency.

'I don't know. Look for yourself.'

'Faaugh!' Disgusted at my non-cooperation, Dame Cecile went to the fridge and opened it. 'There doesn't seem to be much here,' she complained. 'Not for man nor beast.' She rootled farther into its depths and surfaced with a small bowl. 'Do you think she'd eat green beans?'

'Depends on how hungry she is. Try her and see.'

'All right.' Dame Cecile selected a large bean and held it above Cho-Cho's head. 'Sit up!' she ordered. 'Sit! Beg!'

'Cats are different, Cecile. It doesn't work that way, either.' I was cheering up by the minute. It wasn't going to take Dame Cecile long to discover that she and Cho-Cho were incompatible, no matter what her dear Fleur had decided.

Cho-Cho looked unbelievingly at the limp vegetable being held over her head and stalked away. She leaped to the table and sniffed at my coffee.

'You won't like that,' I warned her, 'but have your own drink.' I emptied the cream jug into my saucer and pushed it towards her. 'It will keep you going until we find something else.'

'She's very fussy.' Dame Cecile resumed her seat and regarded us both with dissatisfaction. 'Fleur would have eaten those beans happily.'

'Cats have a palate,' I explained, 'dogs haven't. It's the difference between a gourmet and a glutton.'

'Fleur was not a glutton!'

'I didn't say she was.'

'You implied it!' The choked sob was back in her voice. 'My poor, dear little . . .'

'Where's Eddie?' It was time to distract her. 'He's usually here by now.'

'Evangeline intercepted him. He's driving her somewhere. You didn't think she was going to catch a bus, did you?'

'No, I'd never think that.' I *had* thought her destination might be within walking distance. If she'd commandeered the taxi, she could be going anywhere.

The telephone rang and I waited a few more rings until it became clear that Matilda was not going to answer it herself. I picked up the kitchen extension. 'Hello?'

'Oh, Mother, I'm so glad I've got you. I tried your other number but —'

'I wish you wouldn't, dear. That's Evangeline's mobile. It upsets her to have my calls —'

'So she informed me. At least, I think that's what she was saying. There was so much background noise it was hard to hear.'

'Background noise? Where was she?'

'I don't know.' Martha's tone was bitter. 'But, wherever she was, she sounded right at home!'

'Didn't she — ?'

'Never mind her, Mother. I called you for a consultation. We've had a rather weird recipe submitted and I wanted to run it past you.'

'All right, dear.' I carried the phone back to the table and made myself comfortable. As usual, Martha's voice was so loud and clear that Dame Cecile was able to eavesdrop effortlessly. 'What is it?'

'It's called "When You Bet Your Hat and Lose" and it's a recipe for eating your hat.'

'It must be an old one,' Dame Cecile said. 'No one has worn a hat for decades.'

'You mean a recipe for a hat-shaped cake or cookie, dear?'

'No, an actual hat. For when someone says they'll eat their hat if they're not right — and they're wrong.'

'I can't remember when I last heard that expression.' Dame Cecile was making it a three-way conversation.

'Probably because no one wears hats any more.' I agreed with her on that. 'At least, not that sort of hat. Does it specify any particular sort of hat, dear? Fedora? Bowler? Pork pie? Straw hat? Top hat?'

'Baseball caps are all you see these days,' Dame Cecile put in. 'And the idiots wear those backwards. They'd be better off eating them.'

'Any kind of hat. It doesn't matter. The point is, you burn it down to ashes and then stir the ashes into some food. The recipe recommends oatmeal mixed with maple syrup, but Jocasta thinks —'

'Don't do it, Martha!' Dame Cecile grabbed the phone from me. 'You don't know what they're making hats out of these days. All sorts of synthetic materials are around. Even the fumes might be deadly if you burn them, never mind eating them!'

'And old-fashioned hats probably weren't any better.' I reclaimed the phone to add my caveat. 'They used something terribly nasty to block them. That's where the terms Mad Hatter and Mad as a Hatter originated. The fumes they inhaled all day at their job literally made them insane.'

'Don't even think of using that recipe, Martha!' Dame Cecile took the phone again. 'Not even as a joke. Some fool would be bound to try it — just to show off — and the consequences could be disastrous!'

'She's right, dear.' The tug-of-war with the phone was exasperating, but it had distracted Cecile's attention from her own problems. 'Much safer to leave it out.'

'Yes, I will. I'm so glad I talked this over with you — and Jocasta will be, too. To tell the truth —' a little giggle escaped her — 'neither of us wanted to be the one to test that recipe!'

'One has to be so careful,' Dame Cecile

said as I returned the phone to its shelf. 'I always remember my mother telling me about the World War I cookbook one of the Ministries issued. Naturally, they got some Civil Service type who didn't know anything about cooking to compile it. The emphasis was on not wasting food, so he advised everyone not to waste the leftover rhubarb leaves when they made their pies and desserts from the stalks, but to boil up the leaves and serve them like cabbage.'

'But they're deadly poison!' I gasped.

'Fortunately, someone realized that before the book was distributed too widely. It had to be called back and pulped.'

'Thank goodness for that!'

'Yes.' There was a far-away look in her eyes. 'But I always thought how very useful it might be to know that one could get one's hands on a deadly poison so easily. Just think of it . . . no lies to the doctor to get the right prescription . . . no poison book to sign at the chemist's. Just a quiet stroll down the garden path . . .'

For a blinding instant, I wondered if giving Cecile the role of an eccentric poisoner had been type-casting.

No, no, it couldn't be. She had been with us when Eddie discovered Mr Stuff Yours' body and she could have had no reason to want to dispose of Matilda's new housekeeper. Besides, neither of them had been poisoned. Just the same, I found myself eyeing her warily.

It was with relief that I heard the back door open and turned to see Evangeline and Eddie entering. Evangeline was carrying what looked like a large cardboard cake box — except that it had holes in it and she was struggling to keep a jouncing lid in place. Strange little noises were coming from it.

Cho-Cho pricked up her ears and stalked forward stiff-legged to investigate, almost as suspicious as I was.

'There!' Evangeline set the box down on the table, keeping one hand firmly on the lid.

'What have you got there?' Dame Cecile was also suspicious. 'I don't like the look of that.'

'Don't you?' The box was beginning to rock from side to side now. Evangeline used her other hand to steady it. 'That's too bad, it's for you. I mean, what's inside it is.'

There was a distinct yelp from inside the box.

'No!' Dame Cecile froze. 'You didn't! I can't bear it! No other Peke could possibly replace Fleur!'

'That's just what I thought!' Evangeline

upended the box over Cecile's lap, the lid flew off and the contents tumbled out. It looked like several small black balls of knitting wool . . . wriggling knitting wool.

'What on earth . . . ?' Dame Cecile flinched and stared down at it incredulously. 'What is it?'

It shook itself out and pushed itself up on spindly pom-pommed legs, waving the pom-pom on the end of its tail. Cho-Cho, who had retreated to the safety of my lap, stretched her neck for a closer look, obviously unable to believe her eyes. She turned to blink up at me, twitching her ears.

'*She,*' Evangeline said, 'is a miniature French poodle, with a lineage better than your own. I have her Kennel Club papers in my bag.'

'And you can keep them there!' Dame Cecile fended off the boisterous puppy, who had decided it wanted to lick her nose. 'I'll have nothing to do with this — this *travesty* of a noble animal!'

'They said the fur will grow back out,' Eddie told Cecile. 'You can give 'er a different clip then, maybe one of them lion ones. Might make 'er look more reasonable.'

'So that's where you were this morning,' I said. 'At the kennels.' Suddenly Martha's comment was explained.

'I spent hours choosing the right puppy for Cecile.' Evangeline sighed as Cecile repulsed yet another advance from the pup. 'I thought it was right. Perhaps I should have gone for a Scottish terrier, it might have looked more like a Peke.'

'Oh!' Matilda came into the kitchen. 'Am I the last one up?'

'Probably not,' I told her. 'There's been no sign of Soroya yet.'

'Good!' She moved slowly and unsteadily to a chair. Eddie took one look at her haggard face and rushed to bring her a cup of coffee.

'Matilda, are you all right?' I was concerned.

'I didn't sleep much last night,' she admitted. 'Thank you, Eddie.'

'Toast?' he inquired anxiously. 'Cereal?'

'Nothing, thanks — oh!' The puppy had frisked over to check her out. 'Where did that come from?'

'Need you ask?' Dame Cecile gave Evangeline a disdainful look. Hearing her voice, the puppy pranced back to her and tried to kiss her.

'She likes you best,' Evangeline said persuasively.

'Hmmmph!'

'I've spoken to the police.' Matilda was

still caught up in her own problems. 'They're sending someone over to collect the things we found. I don't know why they want them but —' she shrugged — 'I certainly don't.'

Spurned again, but undaunted, the puppy scurried over to the box it had arrived in and, with a roguish look inviting Dame Cecile to come and play, jumped inside.

'There!' Cecile wasn't playing. In one quick movement, she stood and snapped the lid back on. 'Now get that thing out of here!' She glared at Evangeline.

Cho-Cho quivered in my lap. The ancient call of boxes and bags to felines was exerting its pull. Especially when a small paw groped out of one of the holes before being stopped by its pom-pom. Cho-Cho put one forepaw on the table and watched intently.

The lid popped open and, like a jack-in-the-box, the puppy leaped out, this time carrying something in its mouth. It advanced on Cecile, dangling its prize before her.

'My glove! Where did you get that?' She reached for it and the puppy danced away, delighted at enticing her into a game.

I looked at Evangeline. It was an old trick, but it still worked. She had taken the glove, well-impregnated with Cecile's scent, and shut it in the box with the pup so that it would learn the scent and go to Cecile when it was released.

Cecile managed to catch one finger of the glove and pulled. The puppy hunched down and tugged against her with little growls of excitement.

'Oh, all right!' Cecile let go abruptly and the puppy sat down with a thump. 'Keep it!' She waved a dismissive hand.

The puppy watched her hand, then did a backwards somersault. Taken by surprise, even Cecile laughed.

'Do that again!' Evangeline waved her own hand. The puppy ignored her, bright eyes watching Cecile.

'*Allez-oop!*' Cecile waved her hand again and the pup did another back flip. The little creature was a natural-born clown.

'You can't say that one needs training,' I told her.

'We'll see about that.' Intrigued now, Cecile caught up the wriggling bundle of ecstatic fur, set it down on the floor and walked away from it. 'Heel!' She threw the command over her shoulder.

The puppy did its best. As often in front of her as at her heels, it was firm in its determination not to let her get away from it.

'Well . . .' Cecile strode back to her

chair. 'Well . . .' She sat and the pup promptly leaped into her lap.

'Not bad for such a little one,' I applauded. 'It's still got a lot of growing up to do.'

Sensing victory, Evangeline kept quiet.

'No!' Dame Cecile drew herself up and placed the puppy back in the box. 'No — it's too soon. And it's not Fleur.'

'There was only one Fleur,' I sympathized. Stroking Cho-Cho's little head, I knew just what she meant. 'There can never be another.'

'Never!' she agreed fervently.

Cho-Cho's curiosity was getting the better of her. She wanted a closer look at the strange creature occupying the box she had marked out for her own. Stealthily, she got all four feet up on the table and inched towards the box.

Noticing her approach and thinking it had found a new playmate, the pup gave a joyous yelp and sprang out of the box, charging forward to greet her.

Her fur bristled, her back arched, she hissed and a paw lashed out to strike with deadly accuracy.

The pup retreated yelping and dashed for the sanctuary of Dame Cecile's arms.

'Poor baby,' she cooed, gathering it to her. 'Poor baby, did the nasty cat scratch you?'

Recognizing a good ploy when it saw one, the pup sank against her bosom, whimpering piteously.

Cho-Cho gave it a contemptuous look and took possession of the empty box.

'Poor baby!' Cecile was dabbing at the tiny nose with a lace-edged handkerchief. 'Oh! *Look* at that!' She displayed the hanky indignantly. 'That ruffian cat has drawn blood!'

Really! You could hardly see it. It was barely more than a speck. And you couldn't blame Cho-Cho for defending herself when an unidentifiable creature rushed at her noisily.

'Frou-Frou's blood!' Dame Cecile elaborated.

'Frou-Frou?' She had lost me.

'*Chlo-Chlo, Margot, Frou-Frou —*' Evangeline began humming the song from *The Merry Widow.* Of course! It was a French poodle.

And Cecile had already given it a name, a name that had obviously popped into her head some little while ago. Evangeline and I exchanged triumphant glances. They were bonding nicely.

The sudden pounding at the back door, demanding admittance, broke the pleasant spell.

Chapter Twenty-Two

I didn't like the sound of it — and I was right. Eddie opened the door, then retreated faster than the battered puppy.

A large sheaf of roses intruded into the room. It was beautiful, but I lost any admiration for it when I realized Superintendent Thursby was carrying it.

'Ladies!' he greeted us. 'Forgive my dropping in so informally, but I felt I had to come by and express my appreciation for your wonderful hospitality the other night.' He extended the bouquet to Evangeline.

Oh, yes? If it was such a social call, why were two uniformed police officers — one of them a woman — lurking behind him?

'How kind of you.' Evangeline dropped the bouquet on the table and waited for his next move.

'Also —' He turned to Matilda smoothly. 'I understand you have something for us.'

'Yes.' Matilda stood up slowly. 'I'll get it.'

'Constable Martin will help you.' He

nodded sharply and the female officer moved forward.

'That won't be necessary —' Matilda began.

'No trouble at all, madam. That's what she's paid for.' He nodded again and the woman followed a flustered Matilda from the room. The male constable remained by the door, at ease but watchful. No one was going to get past him.

I told myself that the unsettling thought was ridiculous. Then I looked back at Thursby — Thursby, with the slick vulpine smile that never quite reached his cold eyes — and had an even more unsettling thought: when he left this house, he was planning to take more than the house-keeper's effects with him.

'What are the police doing here?' All the situation had lacked was Soroya and here she was. 'Are they arresting Matilda?'

'Now why would we want to do a thing like that?' Thursby asked innocently.

'Why have you got a policewoman fol-lowing her around?' Soroya countered. 'I met them going up the stairs just as I was coming down. Neither of them spoke to me. What's going on here?'

'Just a little matter of routine,' he assured her. 'It won't take long.' Casually, he strolled over to the cellar door, opened it and looked down. 'You've repaired those steps, I see.'

'You didn't say not to.' Eddie was instantly on the defensive.

'No, I didn't.' Thursby turned and gave Eddie a long look before snapping the wall switch and nodding as the cellar flooded with light. 'New bulb, too, I see.'

'It was dangerous, the way it was.' Eddie backed away and rubbed his wrists as though he could feel handcuffs snapping around them.

'Very dangerous. As was proved.' In the ensuing silence, Thursby seemed to listen for the footsteps overhead.

He had missed his calling. Anyone who could hold their audience so mesmerized belonged on the stage. We could not take our eyes off him.

He closed the cellar door and, with measured tread, came over to the table to stare back at us. He wasn't going to be the one to blink.

Frou-Frou stirred uneasily in Cecile's arms and the sound she made was more whine than whimper. Cecile closed her hand around the little muzzle, quieting it.

'What's that?' Soroya advanced on the table. 'What is that — that — *thing* doing here?'

'It's mine.' Cecile nuzzled the pup. 'My little Frou-Frou. Frivolous Frou-Frou.'

'Well, you can get rid of it! I won't have animals in my house!'

'You have a cat.' Cecile relinquished any claim to Cho-Cho in the light of her new acquisition. 'You can't talk!'

Thursby had gone into freeze-frame mode; only his eyes moved as he looked from one speaker to the other.

Evangeline was also watching, with the slightly puzzled frown she has when trying to decode English crossword clues.

Cho-Cho picked that moment to pop out of the box where she had been crouching and start back towards me, detouring to inspect the roses. Thursby transferred his attention to her.

'Interesting little cat,' he observed. 'I've never seen one like it before. What is it, a failed Manx?'

'Cho-Cho-San is a Japanese bobtail,' Soroya said. 'She comes of an ancient lineage. You can see her ancestors in old Japanese prints and paintings of many centuries ago. They're quite rare in this country,' she added condescendingly.

'Unobtainable, in fact,' Evangeline said under her breath. I realized she had been making efforts on my behalf.

'Is that so?' Thursby nodded sagely. 'That's very interesting. Import her, did you?'

'Not the way you put it, no. I bought her as a kitten when I was touring in the Far East and brought her home with me.'

And gave her to Teddy for an engagement present, then tried to snatch her back when Teddy eloped with Frella. But she wasn't telling Thursby that.

'And no problems bringing her in?' He seemed to sense that there was more to the story than she had revealed. 'No trouble arranging for her six months' quarantine?'

'Oh, the rules had changed by then and she'd had all her shots and proper papers — her Passport for Pets, as they're calling it.'

Cho-Cho gave a sneeze and abandoned the roses. She was close enough to reach now and I gathered her to me. Soroya didn't seem to notice.

'Pretty little thing,' Thursby said dismissively. He looked over our heads and became alert.

I turned to see Matilda and the policewoman returning. The policewoman nodded and I turned back in time to catch Thursby's answering nod. A satisfied, but unpleasant, smile curved his thin lips.

Matilda looked dazed. She moved to the table like an automaton and seated herself between Cecile and me. She kept her eyes downcast, her face expressionless. She might just as well have worn a placard around her neck announcing that something had happened.

'You were right, sir.' The policewoman marched up to Thursby carrying the housekeeper's suitcase. They beamed at each other briefly, radiating self-congratulations.

What was wrong with this picture? Evangeline and I exchanged glances — she felt it, too. Even Cho-Cho sensed the atmosphere; she shivered and shrank against me. Matilda sat with her shoulders hunched, as though expecting a blow. Eddie had all but disappeared into the wallpaper.

'Good work, Constable Martin,' Thursby praised, accepting the suitcase. The large, the very large, suitcase — with no labels at all stuck on it.

That was it! That was not the suitcase we had found!

'What are you doing with my suitcase?' Soroya demanded. 'Give it back to me at once! You have no right — Where did you get it? You've been in my room! How dare you? I'll report you! I'll complain to —'

'They had a search warrant, Soroya,' Matilda said wearily. 'I had to allow Constable Martin to search. She didn't disturb much, she had a pretty good idea of what she was looking for.'

'You little slut! You've always hated me!'

'Not half as much as you've hated me.'

While they were distracted, Thursby set the case on the table and opened it.

Cho-Cho snapped to attention and twisted out of my arms, heading purposefully for the suitcase. She reached it just as Thursby found the catch that released the lid of a hidden compartment.

'No, no, little one.' Thursby pushed her away. 'Mustn't contaminate the evidence. There've been quite a few exotic specimens occupying that space since you did.'

'Exotic species — endangered species!' Evangeline caught on immediately. 'For the taxidermist. Like that golden eagle —'

'Not the eagle, I think,' Thursby said. 'Too large. But quite definitely the hooded cobra. I wonder if she got it from a snake charmer.' He whirled on Soroya suddenly. 'Did you?'

'No!' The denial was automatic, putting it into the *Well, she would say that, wouldn't she?* category. 'I didn't get anything, anywhere. I don't know what you're talking about!' Soroya quivered with indignation. Or was it fear?

'I understand you're in and out of the country a great deal,' Thursby said. 'Filming in all sorts of exotic locations.'

'I am in great demand, yes. Unfortunately, my acting skills are more appreciated abroad than in my own country. It's often the way.' Talking about it seemed to calm her. 'However, Bollywood films are reaching a greater audience now and we're doing more filming in this country. I'm overdue for a breakthrough.'

'You travel with a great deal of luggage.'

'One must consider one's fans. I attend many formal events abroad. That requires a wide selection of costumes. When I'm out of the country, I'm a star. I must dress the part.'

'I'm sure.' Thursby was not impressed. 'And does all your luggage have hidden compartments?'

'I often carry valuable jewellery with me. Naturally, I want to keep it safely near me.' She was overacting. Nothing new with her, I was sure, but something about it tugged at a chord in my memory. I had seen part of this phoney performance before and not in any Bollywood movie.

'And you bring in a lot more jewellery

than you take out!' Evangeline couldn't restrain herself any longer. 'Without paying Customs duty! And it was probably stolen by your cohorts, to begin with!' She turned to Thursby triumphantly. 'I *told* you to look for jewel smugglers!'

'Quite.' He gave her a nasty look. 'Unfortunately for your pet theory, jewellery is a side issue, if it figures at all. Isn't that right, Mrs Jordan?'

Matilda made a small choking sound. I didn't blame her. It was bad enough to have Soroya for a stepmother without anyone rubbing it in.

'I don't know what any of you are talking about!' Soroya blustered. 'And I will not stay here and be insulted!'

'Don't you?' Thursby eyed her coldly. 'If you're not happy here, we can always continue our conversation down at the station.'

'What's she done, then?' Eddie became a little more visible, sensing that he was off the hook.

'I've done nothing!' Soroya flared at him, then turned her fury on Thursby. 'Nothing!'

'Oh, you mustn't be so modest. We think you've done quite a bit, Mrs Jordan.'

Matilda winced.

'We've been keeping a weather eye on Stuff Yours for some time now, in conjunction with the Worldwide Fund for Nature and Customs and Excise. We found you were one of their regular visitors, along with a few other frequent travellers.'

'Never!' Soroya lost colour.

'Every time you returned from a trip, you wasted no time in joining their parade of late-night visitors. You might have been a minor player, but it was a lucrative little sideline, wasn't it, Mrs Jordan?'

'Must you keep calling her that?' Matilda's overstretched nerves snapped. 'Her stage name is Zane. Use that!'

'Oh, yes, that would suit you very well, wouldn't it, Your Ladyship?' Soroya rounded on her. 'I have a right to the Jordan name — I was Gervaise's legal wife! Just as you were his legitimate daughter!'

There was an electric silence. Thursby was smart enough not to break it. He just watched. And waited.

'A very good point.' Evangeline moved in where no one else dared tread. 'Have you encountered many of Gervaise's by-blows?'

'Enough! More than enough! Wretched ghastly creature!' Tellingly, Soroya lapsed into a grotesque parody of an Australian accent: ' "Ooew, you were married to him!

310

Tell me — what was Dad really like?" *Dad!* Ugh!' Soroya shuddered and sketched a push-away motion with her hands. 'The nerve of her! The presumption!'

She might have been carried away by righteous anger, but Soroya was overacting again. Just as she had been when she had pounced first on me and then on Jocasta, pretending that she thought each of us was the new housekeeper. When all the time she knew that the woman was lying dead at the foot of the cellar stairs. Where she had pushed her.

' 'Ere!' Eddie had been following his own train of thought. 'If all those people were watching Stuff Yours, 'ow come you let the owner get killed right under your nose and the place set on fire?'

'We weren't watching it every single minute. None of our budgets are that generous.' Thursby was aggrieved. 'We kept an eye on the place on nights when we suspected a delivery was due.'

'So you tried to pin it on me —' Eddie was no less aggrieved — 'even when you knew there was all these other geezers floating around with a lot more motive.'

'You would have been all right.' Thursby did not have the grace to look embarrassed, but he did seem a bit uncomfortable. 'It's just that if someone thought we were concentrating on you, they'd feel safe and might give themselves away.' He looked pointedly at Soroya.

'She lost her temper with him and hit him over the head with a blunt instrument!' Evangeline was in her element, the better half of *The Happy Couple* doing her stuff again. 'Then she searched the files for any import/export documents he might have kept that would have incriminated her. At some point, she realized that most of the stuffed specimens in the shop were just as incriminating as any papers, so she set fire to the place.'

'I think it's time we went along to the station.' Thursby was not comfortable with audience participation. He nodded to the constables, who closed in on Soroya. 'We have a lot more questions still to ask.'

'How could you?' I had one of my own for Soroya. 'When you rifled those files in the office, you must have seen her. How could you have run away and left poor little Cho-Cho-San to burn alive?'

'I refuse to say another word until I have a lawyer present!' Soroya's mouth snapped shut and stayed that way.

'Well, you're not getting mine,' Eddie said. '' 'E's too good for you.'

Chapter Twenty-Three

It was a relief to get back to the flat in Docklands. Even though it had its drawbacks and we were going to have to leave it shortly, it felt like home. A refuge, however temporary, from the world. Eddie had wanted to return to London and his interrupted life immediately and we had had no hesitation about going with him.

Now we were lounging in front of the glass wall, the riverscape stretched out below us, the clouds turning pink in the glow of the setting sun. On the coffee table, Superintendent Thursby's roses were unfolding, exuding a delicious fragrance.

I made a mental note to gather a handful of the petals when thcy began to fade and add them to the bottle of white wine vinegar for an exotic flavour. Exotic — I didn't want to think about that.

'Anyway,' I said, 'Frou-Frou was a great success. Eventually.' Cho-Cho lounged beside me, safely mine. Soroya couldn't take her where she was going — even if she had wanted her — and a quick telephone conversation with an obliging Teddy had settled the custody question in my favour. I realized that probably meant that I'd have custody of Teddy, as well, at least part-time, but you can't win 'em all.

'Soroya must have been frantic to dispose of the body,' Evangeline said, 'but she couldn't get the chance with Cecile drama-queening around at all hours of the day and night. So the best thing she could think of to do was to pretend that she thought any unknown female was the new housekeeper. She thought that would establish the fact that she believed the housekeeper was still alive somewhere.'

'And those broken stairs had never been a trap set for Matilda or anyone else,' I chimed in. 'Soroya sabotaged them and removed the light bulb after she had impulsively killed her newly discovered stepdaughter. Since she couldn't get rid of the body, she wanted it to look like an accident when it was discovered.'

'I'm not so sure the killing was impulsive,' Evangeline said. 'Soroya was so paranoid, she was probably afraid the woman might make some claim on Gervaise's estate —'

'Which existed only in her imagination,' I sighed.

'Exactly. The house belonged to Matilda

alone — and she could prove it. Gervaise had nothing to leave.'

'Except a heap of trouble for poor Matilda.'

'Oh, well, look on the bright side,' Evangeline said heartlessly. 'Soroya won't have any housing problems from now on. One murder and she might possibly have got a light sentence, but two makes it look as though it was getting to be a habit.'

'That might even be true,' I said. 'If Matilda had died without making a will, then Soroya could have claimed to be her next-of-kin and inherited the house and everything else. And I wouldn't give much for Teddy's chances, either, if Soroya was really getting into the swing of murder.'

'No, even if she plea-bargained with what she knows about the endangered species smuggling —'

The doorbell cut Evangeline off. We looked at each other. We weren't expecting company. Tomorrow, Martha and Jocasta were going to come over early and we were going to spend the whole day cooking up a storm. But tonight was scheduled to be a quiet evening at home.

'Perhaps Martha is bringing over some extra supplies,' I said. 'I'll answer it.' Cho-Cho followed me down the hallway, she

315

didn't want to miss anything.

'Yes? What is it? *Uuurk!*' I opened the door to find myself nose-to-beak with an overgrown feathered monstrosity. Cho-Cho-San took one look, hit high C and skittered back down the hallway, fur bristling.

'What is it?' I repeated faintly, refusing to believe what I was seeing.

'Ah! Trixie! It's Evangeline's investment.' Now I noticed Nigel, standing beside it, tethered to it by some kind of leash. 'I told her I'd see to it that she didn't lose,' he said proudly.

'An ostrich.' I identified it weakly. Several earlier incidents began to make sense. The feather boa . . . the steaks . . . 'You tied Evangeline's money up in an ostrich farm. A failed ostrich farm!'

'Ah, but the assets didn't disappear. Not like dotcoms. These assets are salvageable. I got her share out before the receivers moved in.'

'An ostrich,' I choked. 'You salvaged an ostrich for Evangeline.' The thing stared at me balefully.

'Ah! Not *an* ostrich.' He was wounded. 'I just brought Desdemona up to show you because she's the tamest.'

'She's tame?' The thing raised one foot and stamped it. Then the rest of what he had said registered. 'The tamest?'

'Ah! That's right.' He beamed with triumph. 'I promised her she wouldn't lose — and I kept my promise. There are sixteen more downstairs.'

'Sixteen . . .'

'Trixie!' Evangeline appeared at the end of the hallway. 'Who is it? What's the matter with the cat? She's hiding under the sofa. What is it?'

'Evangeline —' I croaked weakly. 'It's for you.'

About the Author

MARION BABSON was born in Salem, Massachusetts, but has spent most of her adult life in England. She is the author of more than thirty delightful mysteries, including several previous stories featuring the aging movie and stage stars Trixie and Evangeline.